DRUID

A Vancouver Real Folk Story

P.A. WILSON

FREE EBOOK

Claim your copy of Spells and Other Charms when you use the QR code to sign up for my newsletter and learn more about Quinn and Cate's past.

T
he flap of sandals on the stone stairs caught Trahaearn's attention. He turned to see one of the few sane druids descend. Rising, he moved through the gap in the salt circle to speak to the man.

"Why have you come, Gareth?"

Gareth kept his eyes on the ground. Since his spirit and his body had been reunited, he'd acted ashamed. There was nothing he could have done to stop the vampires taking his body, but Gareth carried the blame nonetheless. Trahaearn knew he would be healing that wound for a long time.

"There is a human male at our front door. He keeps knocking, and I fear he will not be ignored," Gareth whispered.

In normal circumstances, Trahaearn would instruct Gareth, and let him deal with the human. These were not normal circumstances, and it would be a long time before any of the druids would be able to deal with anything, let alone a human.

"I'll be there in a few minutes. Do not answer the door. Perhaps he will give up. If not, I will speak with him."

Gareth nodded and turned to climb the stairs. Trahaearn turned to get Dionne's attention. She had completed the circle leaving a generous gate and was waiting for confirmation that she could close it. He walked to where she stood holding the last handful of salt needed to complete the spell. She was glowing a faint amber, not enough to be noticed in full daylight, but enough to show on a rainy day.

He told her about the intruder. "What can I say to him that will send him away without making him more suspicious?"

She thought for a moment and then smiled. "Tell him something that will seem boring. If you let him think there's something interesting inside, he'll keep coming back."

Boring would be easy, Trahaearn thought, I just have to lie.

In the few days he'd been in Vancouver, he'd found a druid grove held hostage by vampires, and an ages old prophecy that exposed the world of magic to humans. Ousting the vampires and freeing the spirits of his druids had been the first step in dealing with the damage from centuries of vampire control in this grove.

He strode up the stairs to confront this human who was interrupting his efforts to get the whole Real Folk world organized to survive the humans. He shoved aside the dread he felt at leaving two relative strangers in the most sacred place in the museum. He had a feeling that allowing others to do magic in his home was the least of the things he'd have to accept in the coming days.

As Trahaearn made his way down the corridor leading to the front door, he heard the thudding of a fist hitting wood. Whoever this human was, he was strong. The doors were solid and thick, having that much of an effect should have taken a hammer. But then, perhaps the vampires had weakened the doors somehow. Another thing he would have to investigate, and more than likely, repair when this crisis was over.

At the door, Trahaearn looked around to make sure none of the druids were wandering the main floor. Most of them simply slept, healing in the comfort of rest, but a few had been found walking in a daze. It would probably be better not to let the human inside anyway. The less he knew about the interior, the less work Trahaearn would need to do to make his lie believable.

He smoothed his robe and pulled the sleeves down to cover as much of his tattoos as possible. He hadn't done any magic, so there was no glow. Taking a deep breath, he arranged his features to an expression that displayed what he hoped would be seen as concern and puzzlement, an otherworldly attitude to match his story.

Before he could open the door, the banging started again. When it was over, he pulled the door open enough to let him walk through, and then closed it behind him. "Is there something I can do to help you?"

There were two men standing too close to him for courtesy. They stepped back and looked him over. Trahaearn watched as they made their minds up. One was a tall man, fat layered over his muscle, bald, and bearded. His companion was short, wiry, and nervous.

The tall one spoke. "We want to know what's going on inside."

"I am brother Trahaearn, and who are you?"

"It doesn't matter who we are. There are weird things going on, and we think you have something to do with it. Staying behind these doors. You're up to something."

So, it had started. The humans knew something was going on and they lashed out at the nearest mystery. "We are up to prayers and meditation. I apologize, but we do not open our doors to those who have not taken orders."

The bald man looked over Trahaearn's shoulder. "How come no one ever noticed you people before?"

Trahaearn looked at the ground, knowing that his meek demeanor would melt, and his arrogance would blaze through if he met the man's gaze. Arrogance was necessary in an arch druid, and came naturally to him. It was not believable in a monk. "I do not know what has changed. We have been here for more than a century." He looked up as he spoke, still avoiding eye contact.

The nervous guy was twitching with impatience. "Just show us inside and we'll go on our way." He stepped toward Trahaearn, but moved back when he realized that the monk was bigger and in better physical condition than he was.

"We are not open to visitors. I must ask that you leave." Trahaearn stood a little taller, keeping his eyes averted from theirs. He tried to convey that he was capable of enforcing the words without being openly aggressive. It was a fine line, and he counted on the robes to add a layer of piety to the act. With most of his druids still in comas from the trauma of their prison, he couldn't let anyone wander the museum.

The bald man grabbed his friend's arm. "Let me do the talking. So, what is the name of your group?"

This man was not as stupid as he first seemed.

"We are monks of the order of Saint David. Our lives are dedicated to prayer for all of the creatures of the earth, for peace, and prosperity. It is time for prayers now, and I must leave you." He turned to reach for the door.

"How many of you are there?" the bald man asked.

"There are twenty brothers here." Trahaearn didn't like the question. Was this man assessing the strength of the opposition if he broke in? It would do him no good. The doors were spelled and only someone who knew the phrases, and had power, would get them open. "We will not answer the door again."

He slipped through the gap and spent a moment inside placing a spell that would deaden the noise of knocking. Then he added a spell to allow him to hear what was going on outside. The voices of the two men became audible as soon as he finished speaking the last syllable. Trahaearn checked the glow on his skin as he listened — the shine was faint but growing.

"We should get a crowbar or something and open it up." That was the nervous man. "There's no way this has been here for a

4

hundred years. I bet it has something to do with the weird glowing. Maybe aliens are in there."

The other man said, "You're crazy. There are no aliens. We need to figure out another way. I think I know someone we can get to help us."

The voices faded as the men left the grove. When he was sure that it was safe, Trahaearn would go and strengthen the protection from the trees. It was not possible to keep people away, but it was possible to have their minds muddled and misdirected enough to make them turn elsewhere.

He looked at his skin again. The glow was not fading. If he did work with the trees, it could be hours before he could go outside again. In this situation, it was more dangerous to be kept in the museum than to be found by the occasional human. And the two men would find them again. Now that they had been in the grove, the misdirection spells would have no effect.

Trahaearn walked to the stairs preparing to join the others in the summoning circle. He knew that this would not be the last time he was left with no choices before the humans were prepared to accept the Real Folk into their world. To live alongside magical creatures, if not peacefully, at least without constant massacres.

In the basement, Trahaearn told Dionne to get ready to close the circle, asked Lionel and Quinn to get in position, and hurried to arrange his thoughts. If they were going to spend time arguing with the other leaders, they might as well begin.

Dionne narrowed the gap and stood with the last of the salt in her hand waiting for the order to complete the spell. "Anyone need to go to the bathroom? Grab a snack? Take a Valium?"

Trahaearn couldn't help the smile that tugged at him with her words. It was too easy to get wrapped up in the dire consequences of the results of the prophecy. A little humor would go a long way to ease the tension. "I think we'll save the mood enhancers for after the conference. In fact, we can crack one of the bottles of wine I found in the cellar as a celebration."

Her face lit up at his suggestion that she was going share in the wine. The human habit of keeping young people from alcohol made it more interesting to them than it should be. He was about to tell her they would water down her glass when the room went icy. No wind. Nothing other than a drop in temperature. Then, the air seemed to blaze with heat.

Trahaearn motioned for Dionne to sit and the others to

remain where they were. Leaving the circle open was safer than trapping them here with something that could be fatal. Anything that could enter through the protections around the museum was powerful enough to do whatever it wanted.

"Who has violated my protections?" Powerful or not, he wasn't going to let it lie without challenge.

A hissing laugh filled the chamber. The heat lessened from a lung blistering level to simply uncomfortable, and the hissing was replaced with shrieks, then silence.

"I am Kali," a harsh voice declared. "I am the bringer of death."

Quinn reached for Trahaearn's hand and muttered, "Don't anger her. We don't know anything about this one. She doesn't sound like The Morrigan."

Trahaearn shook off Quinn's hand. "I am not in the habit of annoying goddesses." He didn't know much about the Kali legend, but he remembered it was violent and bloody. And that she was hard to stop.

"What is it that we can do for you, Kali?"

"Blood. Death." The voice was hollow.

Trahaearn hoped that Kali would be more lucid if he kept asking questions. "We do not conduct blood rites here. Is there something else we can do to please you?"

A glow rose at the opening to the circle. It came with the sound of wailing, and a scent of blood. The glow resolved into a face, strong featured, dark hair, the tongue oddly protruding. "Kill the humans. I want blood. I need the strength it will bring."

This was going to be complicated. Defying the goddess of death was dangerous. Even Quinn had trod carefully around the last one. The Morrigan had, at least, reveled in the two aspects, death and sexuality — or fertility to be precise. This one seemed only to be interested in death. "We have yet to understand the situation. The humans may want to make peace."

A shriek of laughter was the only response.

"Will you give us the time to find our way?" Trahaearn didn't want to promise or refuse anything. "It is too soon for the killing to begin."

A grinding hum replaced the shriek. Then, "I will have blood one way or another. Do not tarry long in your way finding."

Had he just promised to cause a genocide? Trahaearn realized it didn't matter what he'd promised, if Kali thought he was going to kill, she would hold him to it. Another problem he would have to deal with, but not right now. "I will endeavor to reach an understanding before you return."

The shrieking rose in volume until he feared his ears would burst. Then the heat rose until his skin felt like it was blistering, and then the air filled with ice, pulling his breath from his lungs. Just as he was about to collapse, everything returned to normal.

They were alone.

"What the hell was that?" Dionne asked.

"Dionne, stay out of it," Quinn said. "It's beyond your ability to deal with, no matter how many powers you have."

Lionel touched Dionne's arm. "Finish the circle. Even Kali cannot pass salt."

Trahaearn wasn't sure that Lionel was right, but regardless of what Kali could or couldn't do, they still had to try to make peace with the humans. At least there was only one human species. There were twenty types of Real Folk residing just in the Vancouver area.

TRAHAEARN SAT UP STRAIGHTER TO EASE THE STIFFNESS IN HIS back. The discussion was going about as well as he expected. No one agreed, but no one was willing to actually disagree. It was getting harder by the minute to keep the sarcastic comments under control. It felt like the humans would have time to slaughter everyone before any of these people came to a decision. They knew that there had already been a few killings. Some fairies in Romania hadn't hidden quickly enough. The local humans had burned their gardens, and the fairies, in fear of the sudden glow that emanated from the flowers.

Beacon, the sprite who led the forest folk didn't think he had a problem. With all of the fairies, sprites and pixies hidden deep in Stanley Park, he thought no one would find them. Maeve, queen of the sidhe, was certain that they could keep the court invisible. Mark was worried but had admitted that he had no idea how to solve the problem. He had been nominated by the rest of the Real Folk, the ones who had found refuge in Banks', the local Real Folk pub. It made sense, a troll had no way of passing for human, in fact, most of the people trapped there were the same. Those who could pass, had taken the opportunity to find a way home as soon as they could travel.

Dionne was doing her best to explain what might happen, but the fact that she was a witch who could use all of the powers didn't make up for the fact that she was young, and she had been raised by humans. Discovering who she really was and what fate held for her hadn't been as much a shock as Trahaearn expected. Unfortunately, her history was likely to keep her from being an asset in this company. Perhaps it would help when they dealt with humans.

Quinn spent too much of his time defending Dionne, treating her like she was unable to make her own points. Lionel just seemed to be more interested in observing than moving things along. Trahaearn wondered if it was a result of his time in the amulet. Only a few days, but he'd been trapped in that world twice in an effort to serve a prophecy that had dumped the entire Real Folk community into a perilous situation. Why anyone had created that horror of a world inside the Gur amulet was beyond Trahaearn.

He knew that the best way forward was to create a small council who could act for everyone. It was the druid way for good reason. It had worked for centuries. The Arch Druid had a veto, but it was rarely used.

Finally, tired of wasting time, he motioned for Dionne to end what she was saying and let him talk. The look of gratitude on her face gave him a twinge of guilt.

"If we don't form a plan and act, the humans will act first. If we allow that to happen, the best we can hope for is to be tolerated," he said to the images in the circle. "Is that your goal?"

Mark's image slowly shook his head. "I cannot imagine people like me being tolerated. We are not attractive like the sidhe, not useful like the forest folk, or the fairies. Some of us are downright scary."

Trahaearn waited. He needed everyone to state their position. No more waffling. He intended to get them on a path to agreement so he could move on from discussing what they would plan to the actual planning.

"I do not wish to see my people used for their power with plants," Beacon said. Then he glanced to Maeve. "I include the fairies, although I suppose they are your people."

Maeve laughed. "Please do not say that in front of their queens. They consider themselves a people of their own. I am surprised they have agreed to allow you to speak for them."

"Queen Bud is here with me to ensure I do the right thing." He cocked his head as though listening. "She agrees with me. That the humans would use us for their gardens and farms until we are worn to nothing."

All eyes, virtual or physical, turned to Maeve. She was the real challenge to a cohesive approach. The sidhe were beautiful in a way the humans would not be able to resist. They could simply fade into human society, changing location only as it became obvious they didn't age. Magic was a tool that they could put aside.

"I think it is in our interest to live alongside the humans.

There is more opportunity for power that way." She smiled. "And I see what you are thinking, power is what we crave."

That sounded like she would bide her time until the sidhe could control the humans. Trahaearn would let the humans deal with that. His goal was harmony.

"There is one more thing before we move on," Trahaearn said. "We have met our new death goddess." He'd kept the information about Kali out of the conversation until now, knowing that it would distract the participants. But he couldn't expect them to commit to any actions without knowing how different she was from The Morrigan.

Maeve's image moved closer. "Why should that interest us? The Morrigan rarely appeared to us. Well, most of us. She did seem to have an interesting relationship with Quinn."

Quinn blushed and looked down. "I always found it flattering and frightening at the same time. But this new being is not The Morrigan."

"Well, tell us, druid," Maeve commanded. "There is little time to waste on information that does not lead us to a working relationship with the humans."

Trahaearn knew that Maeve would always challenge the council they were creating. It was the nature of a sidhe to rule not cooperate. "This has a direct impact on our plans."

He explained as factually as possible the encounter with Kali. As he did, the echo of her madness seemed to fill the circle.

When he finished, Trahaearn asked Quinn to add anything he'd missed. A druid usually didn't miss details in such matters, but he couldn't take the chance that a nuance had slipped through, one that would make the difference.

"I noticed that the emotions didn't flood us," Quinn said. "When The Morrigan visited, even when I was blind, I felt the rawness of death and of sex. This Kali is a voice and madness, but it did not overwhelm my senses."

Trahaearn asked everyone in the circle, "Do any of you have

knowledge of this being? There must be a legend attached. There always is."

Maeve spoke for the others. "The Morrigan was ancient. I do not remember a time when she was not present. It would be a mistake to assume that all goddesses of death are also ones of fertility, or that each has a legend. The Morrigan was a legend from our homeland. That does not mean that all of these beings will be tied to a Real Folk history."

"I think there's something else, too," Dionne said. "Kali is new. She may be learning her powers like me. It wasn't that long ago that I had no idea there was this whole world, let alone that I was part of it."

It was possible that Kali would grow more powerful, Trahaearn thought. "Let us hope that Dionne is right, and Kali's madness diminishes as her power grows."

"Time is passing, druid," Maeve said. "What else do you wish to achieve?"

A good question. Trahaearn knew the long game he was playing was to get the Real Folk more than surviving this change, but what was he still missing from this gathering? Perhaps it was simply commitment. "If we are all agreed that the goal is to find a harmonious way to live among the humans, then I think we are done for the moment. Otherwise I fear we will inadvertently provide Kali with her wishes."

Each of the attendees agreed that they would work toward harmony. Maeve, as expected, did not just leave it there. "I think, druid, we need to agree on the authority we all have. I am not willing to cede anyone the authority to place a yoke on my court, but I do see that we need a leader. None of us wish a return of the witch trials when humans can't tell a witch from a sprite. Nor do we wish a second massacre like what happened to the vampires. If we are to speak for the entire world of Real Folk, we must not bicker amongst ourselves."

"Queen Maeve, please feel free to call me by my name. I'm

sure you wouldn't want anyone to refer to you as sidhe." It was a risk to speak to her that way, but Trahaearn couldn't help hearing a level of distain when she called him druid. Knowing that it reflected the previous inhabitants of the druid bodies didn't help him accept it.

Maeve's image narrowed her eyes. Whether in seduction or warning, Trahaearn couldn't tell. Nor could he decide which to fear more. "Very well, Trahaearn. Now what authority will we hold in your new world?"

It didn't feel right to be answering that question. It wasn't so much that he couldn't take control, that's what his job was as arch druid. But he didn't think they would let him take it without assigning any blame. Even blame for problems that they caused. "Perhaps we should all say what authority would be acceptable?"

Beacon snorted. "I am prepared to hand over any authority. I only ask that no one sell my folk into slavery, but that does not need to be said."

"You can make deals for those who are at Banks', but we will want to vote on it." Mark's words came out in a grind of stone against stone.

Trahaearn waited for Maeve to speak, hoping she would be reasonable, but Dionne spoke first, "You can make decisions for me."

Lionel echoed her words.

Annoyed at everyone's willingness to be led, Trahaearn turned to Quinn. "Are you crazy enough to agree? Since you are the only wizard left in the area who hasn't handed me far too much power, will you draw the line this side of insanity?"

Quinn laughed. "I'm surprised that you are fighting this so hard. I will let you guide our decisions, but not make them."

A warm laugh filled the circle. Maeve was finally adding her opinion. "I think you need to take the lead, druid. It is only you or I who are capable, and no one will trust me. Now that you have our words, what do you propose?"

He wasn't going to buckle under. This was too important for egos and games. Only a true council would work. "I propose we work as a small group; we make plans, and we make decisions together. It works for the druids; it will work here."

"How many of us would be in the council?" Beacon asked. "Unless Quinn is joining, there are four of us, and that is not practical. We need a fifth, or any odd number to ensure we have a tie breaker."

Trahaearn was torn. He wanted to bang their heads together. If they couldn't agree quickly on the makeup of the council, how would they ever make a deal with the humans? It had been a little more than a day since the glow had happened and it was only a matter of time before they would lose the thin advantage they had. The Vancouver area was populated with more Real Folk than any other place in the world. It made sense that these people lead the effort to build an accord with the humans. He only hoped that the humans would be as willing to agree as a people as the Real Folk were.

An old lesson came to him as though his teacher were in the circle with them. *There is always time to slow down, but never time to repair haste.*

"We need to take a break. I will consider what you have said, and I will have an answer for you when we come back together. Shall we say a half hour?"

Maeve smirked, an odd expression for such a delicate and regal face. "We are yours to direct, Trahaearn." Her image flickered and then disappeared.

The other images simply disappeared with no comment.

Dionne stood and stretched. "Do you want me to break the circle?"

He nodded and she brushed the salt aside with the toe of her boot.

"I need to be alone to think. I will not be long. You may want to find food."

❧ 3 ❧

T he druid was gone.

It was time to bring the others who were in the room to her side. It was clear to Kali that the druid was not going to start the slaughter that she needed. He did not understand that she had to grow her power. Only when she was strong could she use the other aspects of that power. Death was the most powerful, and she could only grow it through mass killings. This drip of life from the normal deaths did not even let her appear to the beings of this realm. She was weaker now than when she arrived. It would not be long until she faded away.

The girl was likely to be her best target. She looked young enough to believe Kali's stories, and yet old enough to hold strong anger.

"Girl," Kali whispered, or at least she had aimed for a whisper. The girl's reaction made Kali wonder if it was a roar.

"Go away," the girl said, her voice strong and defiant.

Good. Defiance was a form of anger. Kali could twist it to her aims. "I need you. I need your friends." The others were listening. The older man reached for the girl's arm to stop her speaking. If

Kali was in her full power, she would have stopped the man's heart, but she could not do that yet.

"Dionne, do not speak to her until we are more sure of her nature." His words held the power of a teacher.

Kali couldn't fight against the bond she recognized between the two. The other one, the younger man, might be willing. There was a shadow on his spirit that Kali could use to inveigle him to her side. "Boy, I beg of you to help me survive." Men were more easily trapped if they thought they were helping.

"My name is Lionel, and I will not assist you. If all you want is blood, you must look elsewhere." He turned back to smoothing the soil that formed the floor of the room.

Rage drained Kali.

These were mortals, and they should not have the power to deny her.

Her time in this room was limited. Kali needed to find death somewhere to recharge. When that was done, she would have her way. She sent her senses out to find the pool of red mist that told her a violent death had occurred and it was time to feed. When she came into her full power, she would draw that mist to her, now she had to go where the killing was being done.

"I will not be denied. You have time to rethink your allegiance, but I will have death. I will gain my power, and I will have my way."

TRAHAEARN FOLLOWED LIONEL DOWN THE STAIRS. IT HAD ONLY been minutes since he'd left, not enough time to consider his options, but apparently enough time for a crisis to occur. "What actually happened, Lionel?"

"You need to talk to Dionne. It started with her."

Trahaearn wondered at how easily Kali slipped into his home. She hadn't appeared anywhere but in the basement, where the earth was bare, but it didn't mean any other place was safe. If she got to his druids before they became fully sane, she might gain purchase. And if his druids were dragged into any kind of madness again this soon after being rescued from the amulet, he despaired of ever healing them completely.

In the room, Quinn was scattering seeds at the base of the walls that formed the outer circle. Dionne was sitting with her hand on the soil, her eyes closed. As soon as he stepped off the stone of the stairs and onto the soil, Trahaearn felt her presence.

She must have felt his because she opened her eyes, stared directly at him, and said, "I don't know how she's getting in. The earth is clear. There is no taint of a spell that would allow her to violate the protections."

Trahaearn sat beside Dionne and placed his hand on hers to feel how she was testing the dirt. The earth was pure, and there should be no way for any being to penetrate uninvited. But Kali was unknown, and that was more worry to him than the demands for blood. "We will figure it out, but we have more important considerations to deal with. Until Kali actually gets her way, we can put her at the bottom of the list. In fact, if we do not resolve this situation, and find a way to live with the humans, she will get what she wants and more."

Dionne removed her hand and dug into her pocket. Pulling out her phone, she stared at the screen. "No bars. If we have time before we reconvene, I can do some searching for information on Kali. There might be something online. I'll have to go upstairs to get a signal."

She looked at Quinn as well as Trahaearn. He felt sympathy for her. As her teacher, Quinn should have the last word, but they were in Trahaearn's home, and that gave him power. Her confusion also gave him an idea. "If you are okay with that, Quinn, perhaps you and I can talk while these two do research."

Quinn nodded to Dionne and Lionel to go upstairs. When they were alone, he said, "You want something?"

Trahaearn smiled, Quinn may have been less willing to take

the lead, but he was intelligent and perceptive. "I think we need someone outside of the museum who can pass among the humans. To take information to the other groups. Someone who has a good relationship with Maeve and Beacon."

"And you want Dionne to do that?"

Trahaearn could see the argument forming on Quinn's face. He did still think of her as a new witch, rather than a powerful one with a lot of street wisdom. "I propose you leave Dionne and Lionel here, to work with me. They work better as a team. I meant you to act the liaison. If you don't have enough charms to avoid doing actual magic, you can stock up today. That will mean you are available for the others by nightfall when your glow fades sufficiently."

Quinn's eyes lost their focus as he thought through the suggestion. Then he nodded. "I'm not sure about having a good relationship with Maeve, but I guess I'm as close as anyone will be to that. We can set up a message drop between this space and my workroom. I'll try to keep everyone calm and patient, and not making their own side deals."

Relief calmed Trahaearn. He'd been preparing a strong argument to get his way, but Quinn was a realist, and that saved time.

"There's one thing," Quinn said. "I need you to promise me that you will keep them safe. I am responsible for Dionne, and even though Lionel is a full wizard, he only became one a few days ago. And that was after he was trapped twice in the amulet. He needs protection."

Trahaearn agreed, and he would do his best, but if it took sacrifice to save the Real Folk, he would give up Dionne and Lionel. He knew, too, that they would gladly jump off a cliff to do it if they thought it was needed.

"Hey, check this out," Dionne called as they both appeared at the turn in the stairs. "There's tons of stuff on Kali."

Trahaearn knew that information online was often made up,

but he couldn't stop the surge of hope that they would have an advantage over Kali. "What did you find?"

Dionne held out her phone. "I didn't read it, just downloaded it so we could all see it off-line." She turned the phone to touch something on the screen. "What the hell?"

Trahaearn reached for the phone. There were words on the screen, but they were disappearing as if something was eating them. "How is this possible?"

Dionne took the phone back and stared at it as if she could memorize the information before it disappeared. "Someone could have written a program to delete all information on Kali from the internet. It's been done before. But it shouldn't take anything from my phone." She looked up at him. "I'm sorry. There was a ton of information."

Trahaearn beckoned everyone to the circle again. "There will be physical books. When we have the opportunity, we can search the human libraries for this information."

He told Dionne to reform the circle. It was almost time to meet with the others again. As she started her walk, the sound of sandals on stone announced Gareth's arrival.

"Another of the humans is knocking."

Trahaearn rose. "Keep preparing. I will send this one away too." He followed Gareth from the basement, trying to work out how he could prepare if humans kept trying to speak to him. It would be a boon when the council agreed on a structure, but now, it was simply another danger, another delay.

This time when he opened the door, Trahaearn wasn't facing someone who looked angry. The man waited a few feet from the door, giving a polite distance for a conversation. He was tall and built light, with a slight stoop to his shoulders. Trahaearn recognized the posture as that of someone who was constantly bent over books or some other work.

The man was dressed in stylish clothes, and wore them like a costume. His eyes were bright with interest. He stepped forward, hand out to shake. "Jacob Meyers. I work for the local paper. I wonder if we can have a chat."

Trahaearn couldn't spend any of his scant time with the news media. He'd seen enough of their work in California. The truth wasn't just a casualty in their thirst for scandal, it was the first sacrifice. He stared at the hand, hoping his rudeness for not shaking it was enough to put the man off the scent. "I am busy at the moment."

Jacob's smile remained fixed as he dropped his hand and took out a notepad. "I only have a few questions. This monastery has been hidden until the last few days. Given everything else odd happening, I wondered if it was connected to the glow?"

Trahaearn looked blankly at the reporter. "What happens in the world is of no interest to us. Now, I must get back to the brothers. We are about to enter a time of meditation."

Jacob's eyes narrowed just a fraction and then his expression opened again. "Perhaps I should have made an appointment, but if you don't speak to me, you will be approached by other reporters, some of them won't be as interested in the facts as I am."

The idea of a barrage of reporters knocking on the door made Trahaearn reconsider. No one who wasn't invited could get through the doors — well, no one except for Kali. But he couldn't be sure that none of the druids would be tricked into inviting humans. If he had to speak to reporters, perhaps this one would be his best hope for controlling the message.

Just not now.

"Would you be willing to return in an hour? I can make sure that we will be uninterrupted." He hoped that Kali would be invisible and inaudible to humans, but that internet issue was worrying. The world was changing in more ways than just the glow of magic.

Trahaearn saw conflict on the reporter's face. He wanted the story, and he wanted control.

Jacob finally smiled and said, "An hour. I can keep this away from my colleagues until then." He reached out his hand. This time Trahaearn took it and shook.

He watched until Jacob disappeared through the trees before crossing the clearing to the edge and touching the trunk of the nearest tree. Their magic should keep out the casual wanderer. The fact that someone had breached the circle of trees twice in such a short period of time was odd — more than odd, worrying.

He sank his senses into the tree, feeling the power and vitality of ancient life. The magic was still there, still strong, still working. It would bear deeper investigation when they had time, but for now he would be more careful, and perhaps, Quinn could drop a few distraction charms to reinforce the trees.

IN THE BASEMENT AGAIN, TRAHAEARN MOTIONED FOR DIONNE to close the circle and to the others to take their places. He told them about his encounter with Jacob while they waited for Maeve, Beacon, and Mark to rejoin them. "Dionne, I would like you to observe the meeting and advise me."

"Sure. Um, Quinn told us we were going to stay here, so where am I going to sleep? And I need to get some of my stuff from Quinn's." She poured the last of the salt to close the circle as she spoke.

"We can arrange a private room for you, and maybe Quinn can bring your things. I don't want you to be seen on the street until we are ready." Trahaearn glanced at Lionel. He didn't seem to have any requests, but that couldn't be true. "Lionel, what else do you need?"

"A change of clothes would be nice. Maybe I can go with Quinn and get our stuff."

He didn't want either of them out of his sight, but it wasn't reasonable. "Fine. Dionne, will you give them a list?"

She giggled. "Yeah."

Trahaearn worried that Lionel would still be blushing over the list when the crisis was over. He was about to comment on it when images filled the circle in front of them.

"Well, druid?" Maeve said. "We have discussed our position and we are united. Our expectation is that you will take the lead and find a way for us to thrive."

He had hoped they would come around to his point of view, but there was no doubt in Maeve's voice. Mark and Beacon watched her, obviously in agreement. It was an unfamiliar position for Trahaearn, to be arguing against taking the lead. Was he truly trying to be diplomatic, or was this fear?

There was no time for reflection. If they were adamant that he do this, then he would. "I will expect you to stand back and let me do as I think best for all the Real Folk." The three images nodded. "I will provide you with information, and I will not bind you to an agreement without consulting you." He couldn't let this be done with simple nods. He would always be second-guessing their commitment. He would always be worried that Maeve would be working in the best interests of the sidhe, regardless of the other Real Folk.

"I need you to say that you agree and be bound by the power of this circle." Something flashed in Maeve's expression. Was it anger? Trahaearn watched closely as Maeve got control of her emotions. What he saw was fear. Maeve was afraid of what was happening. It wouldn't last, but it gave him hope that she would stand by her words.

Mark spoke first. "I agree on behalf of the people I am protecting that you will lead us on this matter."

Then Beacon. "You stand as my agent in this matter."

Finally, Maeve spoke, the fear gone from her face and her voice, "In the matter of finding a working relationship with the humans, you have the authority that I hold over my people."

Trahaearn took in a deep breath and used magic to seal the agreement, barely enough to cause a glow. "So be it."

The three images disappeared.

Quinn told Dionne to clear the circle so they could go upstairs.

Trahaearn saw that she was glowing brightly; it would be hours before it faded. He looked at his hands. The glow was faint. It would be gone before his meeting with Jacob.

❦ 4 ❧

The small room that Trahaearn used as an office, or would when the museum was finally restored, would do for the meeting with Jacob. It had the added benefit of a listening closet in the back. A place where a druid could sit and hear everything that went on. It was concealed enough that the brilliant glow from magic Dionne had used to cast the circle wouldn't shine through.

When she was inside, Trahaearn said, "Do not try to speak. I want your opinions and I will ask you to come forth if I need you to be seen. Just listen and trust that I know what I am doing."

"Okay, but don't you want my advice?" Dionne wiped off the seat before she lowered herself. The dust rose and then settled back. She focused and suddenly the room was clear of dust. "Sorry, I didn't want to end up sneezing. The spell won't make much difference to how much I shine."

"When we have this settled, maybe you can cast the spell on the entire museum." He dreaded the thought of the time and effort that it would take to bring the museum back to the pristine state that it should be in.

"Only works in small spaces. I sent the dust to the basement. I figured dust and earth were close enough to the same thing."

Trahaearn shrugged. "I guess it's a good thing that physical work calms the effect of magic. Now, here's what I plan." He didn't want her rushing out to save him if she thought he was doing something wrong.

When he finished explaining, she settled herself comfortably and said, "It should work."

Suppressing the lecture that rose at her words, the one any druid would have had about respecting elders, Trahaearn returned to the office. While he waited, he tidied the books in piles that leaned against the walls. The reporter would see only a study for a monk who had retired from the world.

Jacob knocked on the museum door exactly when he had agreed. Trahaearn heard Gareth greet the man. The door to the study opened and Jacob stepped through. He looked the same as before with one exception; he held a camera in his left hand. That wasn't going to be okay.

"Brother Gareth, please take the camera and put it in a safe place while I speak with our guest."

The human looked at the equipment and seemed to consider arguing. If he insisted, Trahaearn would take the opportunity to end the conversation. He needed to get away from the museum and find some contacts. If this Jacob was not useful, he was just an obstruction.

"Please be careful with it. I need it in my work."

Gareth took the camera and held it as though it was made of excrement. After looking at Trahaearn for permission, he left them alone, or at least alone by Jacob's point of view.

Trahaearn relaxed in the chair, hoping to put Jacob off his guard. "You wanted to ask questions? Please start. I will answer what I can."

The man pulled a notepad from his backpack. A pencil was jammed through the spiral coil binding. He sat and mimicked

Trahaearn's pose. "You are aware that there has been a change in the world. There are areas where an unnatural glow emanates. People who try to locate the cause find themselves lost or in unexpected locations without knowing how they arrived."

Trahaearn steepled his fingers. Not answering, because Jacob had simply made a statement. If Trahaearn took it as a question of his knowledge, then the reporter would dig in to that topic. It would be a verbal battle to get what Trahaearn needed — an assessment of the man's ability to accept the unbelievable.

"Your abbey?" Jacob raised an eyebrow asking for confirmation of the label.

Trahaearn nodded and continued to wait.

"It appeared, or seemed to, at almost the same time as the glowing started. It occurs to me that my source has a point. There must be a connection."

"Your source is the man who interrupted our meditation earlier." If there were others making the connection, it was vital that Trahaearn know before things got out of hand.

Jacob looked down at his notebook. Trahaearn knew that action. The man was stalling, trying to decide how little he could admit and still gain the trust of the person across from him. Given Jacob's age, and actions, Trahaearn had no doubt that he was up-and-coming rather than experienced as a reporter.

Jacob tapped his pencil on the page and then looked up. "I don't usually share the identity of my sources. Since you are a man of the cloth, I will confirm your statement, but I won't tell you the man's name or anything else."

This human had promise, but his attempts at being in control revealed that he was inexperienced. Trahaearn's tension left him, his emotions mirroring his outward appearance of calm. Jacob would be a good contact to the world of humans. But revealing the knowledge of the Real Folk could change that.

Jacob leaned forward, clearly noting the change in Trahaearn's manner. It would be good to remember that immaturity didn't mean incompetence. Trahaearn felt a touch of caution dim his optimism.

"Let's not dance around this," Jacob said. "You know something. If you didn't, you would have told me to get lost. Okay, maybe in nicer words. So why won't you tell me?"

Trahaearn wanted to trust the directness, but he knew that Jacob couldn't possibly be anticipating the answer. "What do you think is going on?"

"So, you do know, and it's truly out there." Jacob closed his notebook and rubbed his face. "Why have you been hidden all this time?"

The answer to that would be a distraction, Trahaearn thought. "We have not been hidden from those who need us." Not exactly true. The Real Folk had known about the museum, but the druids had been absent. "Tell me what you think has happened."

"There's been a lot of crap going on. Maybe a virus. Something that is keyed to DNA?" He looked at Trahaearn but when there was no confirmation, he continued, "Weirder than that? Hmm, aliens? No, vampires?"

Before Jacob could continue with his list of crazy ideas, or maybe it was the mention of the vampires, Trahaearn held up his hand to stop him. "What do you want out of this? It is not just a story, I think. Tell me your plans."

Jacob straightened and crossed his arms over his chest. "Whatever it is, I want to be the one who breaks the story. I know it's not just local. I know it won't be long before the networks get it, but I want to do it right. I want to give the facts. I see it as an opportunity to solve a problem. The others will see it as an opportunity to improve ratings, which usually means spreading fear and hate."

Trahaearn could see the conviction blazing out of Jacob's stare. It almost had a power like magic. The man truly believed what he said. It might be naive, but Trahaearn needed that passion. "And what if the truth is so out of your experience that you cannot believe it?"

A frown crossed Jacob's face.

Trahaearn suppressed a smile. The man was probably only in his twenties; what kind of experience could he have to compare this to?

To his credit, Jacob considered for a few minutes before speaking. "I don't know what could be so odd that I couldn't believe it. Or that it couldn't be proven somehow. I do know that there is no way for me to unlearn something, or to un-see something, so what will you do if I can't take in what you tell me?"

There was fear in Jacob's eyes now. He hadn't asked if he would be killed to keep the secret, but it was apparent that he wondered. Trahaearn would not have to resort to that. There were a number of spells that would cause Jacob to forget what he'd seen, but it wouldn't come to that because the spells couldn't be targeted to specific memories. If he really meant what he'd said about getting the truth out, then he could be trusted. And there was no doubt in Trahaearn's mind that Jacob meant it now. Would it hold when he realized that many of the things that terrorized children were real: trolls, kobolds, ogres?

Dionne was going to be Trahaearn's proof, and she wasn't a living bogeyman. Her glow would still be strong. She was doing a great job of being silent. Trahaearn hoped that it didn't mean she'd fallen asleep, because he needed her view on what happened. He wished he could take a break to ask her advice, but this moment would not last. Jacob was eager now. The lingering doubt in Trahaearn's mind was not about Jacob, but about his profession. In California, he'd observed the way the media could descend like a pack of hyenas. Not concerned about truth, as Jacob had said, but about their own appearance of importance. The people who were attracted to reporting seemed to be either earnest seekers of truth, or self-aggrandizing walking egos.

If Jacob were one of the Real Folk, Trahaearn would ask him

to take an oath, but he didn't know if an oath had the same power over a human. The man was looking at him, waiting for answers. That patience would not last. Even if an oath had no power, it was worth the try.

"Before I tell you the cause of this change, and what needs to be done, I need you to swear that you will work with us, or you will keep silent." That oath was the simplest and if it worked, the human would find his voice gone if he tried to violate it.

Jacob shook his head without pause. It made Trahaearn worry that he'd made an error in trusting the passion he'd seen in the man.

"That's too open for me to just agree," Jacob said. "I need to know that I'm not promising to assist the next genocide, or the collapse of civilization."

Relieved that the request was so reasonable, Trahaearn said, "Fair enough. I swear to you that far from causing either of those things, we are working to avoid them." He stood and found a blank sheet of paper that was imbued with a sealing spell. Trahaearn placed it on the table. For Real Folk, speaking the words would be sufficient to seal the oath. Trahaearn thought that putting ink on paper and signing it would be enough like a pact to seal the word of a human.

"We will write it as a simple contract. I will swear that I am not asking you to become the ally of the next Hitler, or Attila the Hun, or Investment Banker. You will swear to work with us, or to keep silent. Will that be acceptable?" He willed Jacob to agree. No magic, he couldn't risk a glow, just hope.

Jacob still seemed reluctant to commit. Trahaearn knew that he would feel the same way if their positions were reversed. It didn't help that he kept assigning motives, which were unlikely to be real, to the delay. Schooling himself to patience, something he hadn't required for years, Trahaearn waited for the man to work through his own doubts. This was too important to rush, too important to get wrong.

"Fine," Jacob said finally. "We have to trust at some point. Write it out and I'll sign."

Trahaearn took a pen from the desk drawer and wrote the contract. Jacob signed, and reached out his hand to shake. It was an opportunity that Trahaearn couldn't pass up. Now that the oath was taken, a small probe into Jacob's mind would seal the decision before it was too late. The glow would probably be imperceptible. He took Jacob's hand and gave it a firm shake. The probe he sent confirmed that Jacob was committed. With luck that commitment would survive the disclosure.

"I think it would be better for you to sit," Trahaearn said. "I will show you rather than try to explain."

Jacob sat and tried to look worldly, to express that there was nothing that Trahaearn could show him that would overturn his understanding of the world. Trahaearn could see the eagerness shining through the nonchalant front, eagerness and a touch of fear. It made him feel better that Jacob was not so jaded that he truly was unshockable.

"Dionne, please join us," Trahaearn asked.

The glow she emitted was visible as she turned the corner and entered the short hall into the office space. Jacob jerked up straight, his eyes wide. He leaned away as though she was contagious — a reasonable assumption.

"Don't worry, it's not catching," she said with a smile.

"What is it?" Jacob asked.

Trahaearn looked to Dionne and motioned for her to answer.

"Magic. It's real magic," she said. "I know. I wouldn't have believed it before. But, well, maybe we need to show him some actual spells."

Trahaearn wasn't ready to suffer the effects of doing magic yet. First, Jacob needed to believe in the magic, and then to see the effect. "What spell would work best?"

She laughed. "If we could get a fairy here, or a sprite it would be better. But you know Bud won't come near a human even if she could travel."

Jacob stood and moved closer to Dionne. "Are you saying that fairies exist? Come on. I'm not that stupid."

Dionne glared at him. "You think we would play games after all that?" She gestured to her body. "This isn't a joke. If I could stop doing magic, I'd be fine, but the fairies can't because they are made of magic." She seemed to reconsider her anger. "Fine, here's a spell that might convince you." She reached out her hand and created a perfect image of Bud on her fingertips. "Go ahead and touch it."

Clearly looking for the trick, Jacob reached out a finger and poked at the image. He jerked back when his finger hit resistance. "Not a hologram." The wonder in his voice was clear. Then he straightened, gathering cynicism around him like a cloak. "Any Vegas magician could do that. You had it hidden."

Dionne looked at Trahaearn for guidance. "It was easier for me, because I felt the magic when Lionel did it. And I could do some right away. What do you think I should try next?"

Trahaearn looked at Jacob before asking, "What would make you believe it is real?"

"Can you read my mind?" The words were tinged with fear, but to his credit Jacob was still trying to believe.

"No, and I don't know any Real Folk who can." Dionne paced the small room.

"Real Folk?" Jacob asked.

Trahaearn watched Dionne, worried that she'd try to do something dangerous to prove her point.

She stood still and answered, "We call ourselves that. The Real Folk, those with magic, those who have been here so long we are part of your childhood stories."

"I'm not saying I believe you, but there are different kinds, right?"

Trahaearn nodded, feeling more secure in teaching mode. "I

am a druid. Dionne is a witch. You'll eventually meet more of us if we can help you believe."

Dionne stopped pacing. "I know. Are you allergic to bees?" she asked Jacob.

"No, why, —" his words were cut off as the room filled with bees frantically trying to find a way out of the room.

Jacob batted at them as though that would save him from a vicious attack.

Dionne waved her hands and the bees disappeared. "Believe me now?"

Jacob reached behind him for the chair and sat heavily. His breathing had sped up to the point where Trahaearn feared he would faint from hyperventilation. As Trahaearn approached to help, Jacob waved him off. "I guess I have two choices. I can believe what you are telling me, or I can accept that I've gone crazy."

Dionne smiled. "You might wish you were mad by the time you meet the rest of us. So, can you see how much more I glow now, or do you need more proof?"

Trahaearn was ready to cast a small spell if Jacob couldn't see how Dionne blazed with amber light where she'd only glowed before.

"No, I can see it. Man, I wish I had that on video."

Trahaearn's muscles relaxed. The man believed in the existence of magic. Now they would learn whether he would be afraid, or he would help. Trahaearn still had no plan, Dionne hadn't had time to help him form one, and now he realized how much easier the next step would be if he knew what that step was.

Jacob reached out to Dionne, stopping just short of touching her. "May I?" he asked.

At least he was behaving like she was a person and not a demon. Dionne made the connection, taking Jacob's hand and placing it on her exposed arm.

"See, it's just a glow. I'm not hot, or anything." She stepped back when Jacob lifted his hand.

Trahaearn pulled a chair from the corner so she could join them. "I'm sure you didn't even suspect this was the answer." He needed to feel out Jacob's reaction. The man may say he wasn't like the reporters who chased sensational headlines, but perhaps he wasn't tested yet, and the oath might not hold.

Jacob shook his head, still in a daze. "I'm pretty sure you can keep this secret for a while, but someone will eventually find out. You say there are fairies and other creatures."

The word raised Trahaearn's protective nature. Would Jacob's help dissolve when he realized that the other creatures didn't look human? "They are people, not creatures. But yes, most of your human mythology exists. In this area, we have mainly the western myths, fairies, sidhe, a troll, sprites, imps, pixies." There were more, but he didn't want to overwhelm Jacob. "What can you do to help?"

Relaxing in his seat, and rubbing his hands through his hair, Jacob didn't answer. Trahaearn could see the thoughts chase themselves through the man's mind in his furrowed brow and tight lips. Dionne leaned forward to speak, but Trahaearn motioned for her to be patient. Jacob needed to think this out for himself.

Eventually Jacob leaned forward again. "You need allies in place before we go public. You need to do that soon, because people are going to make it into the park where that glow is showing. If the wrong people find you before you declare yourselves, you'll be fighting all their prejudice and greed, but if we get you the right support, you can control the message. People will have a side to take other than the haters. It won't be easy, but it will be possible."

It was encouraging to have Jacob state what Trahaearn had known to be the right move. He still didn't know how to implement it, but they needed to control the message. "What allies?"

"That's tricky. You need people with some power, and people with some integrity. I have a couple of names in mind, but I can't guarantee that they won't be in it for themselves."

Trahaearn heard Dionne chuckle and felt a smile grow on his own face. "Everyone is in it for themselves. The right people will see that we can all benefit together. The wrong people will try to benefit on our downfall. Who do you suggest?"

"How much do you know about the politics here?"

Trahaearn turned to Dionne. "I haven't been here long enough. Dionne, tell me what you know."

She scratched her neck as she thought. "Okay, the cities around here all have their mayors and councils. They all kind of act individually and together. It's the Metro Vancouver area, but lots of stuff is still just Vancouver, or Richmond, or whatever."

"Yeah, she's right, it's complicated, but that works in our favor. I know two people on Vancouver council who have influence on the other city councils. Good influence so far. And they have connections federally. If we can get them on board, then we have the strength we need to start." He nodded as though he'd convinced himself of the plan.

"So, what's the problem?" Trahaearn asked. "I know there is one."

Jacob shrugged. "They're politicians. They'll be looking for their angle. They'll want some power out of it. I don't know, but I'm guessing they'll want to represent the magical people."

"The Real Folk," Dionne corrected. "We are called the Real Folk."

"That might be a problem," Jacob said, twisting his mouth in a painful grimace. "I'm pretty sure we'll have people focusing on the fact that we humans think of ourselves as real folk too."

Trahaearn knew that semantics could be as dangerous as weapons. "We'll find a way to deal with that, at least around humans."

"Shall I make arrangements?" Jacob asked.

Trahaearn rose and gestured for Jacob to pack his notebook into his backpack. "Yes, we can meet this evening if that is possible for your contacts. Do not tell them anything, allow us to reveal the truth."

Jacob shoved the notepad into the bottom of his pack. "How will I let you know?"

Dionne gave him her phone number. "Don't screw this up, please. These people are my friends, and my family. I don't want anyone to die."

Looking like he knew how easily things could turn deadly, Jacob nodded.

5

Kali experienced nothing but darkness. Here, sound was her strongest way to sense direction. It was only when she made contact with a soul on the world, did she see anything. The druid was proving too hard to influence. It would take more power than she currently had to bring him to her way of thinking. There must be someone outside this veil of darkness and noise.

Sound was not the only thing that happened here. Kali got hungry as well. The wail of pain from some human tragedy pulled at her, the souls almost ready to pass, almost ready to leave their residual power in her as they died. She would gain a little, too little, substance and they would go to their next level. If she didn't get enough substance soon, she feared that whoever sent her here would move her to a place even worse.

She drifted toward the sound of despair, hoping it would do more than just sate her for a few moments. After absorbing the energy, Kali tried to focus on the sounds around her before hunger forced her to seek dying souls. It took too long, took too much energy, but she heard a conversation before the screams of dying children pulled her away.

"You need to find out what this is about. This is not God's work," the voice said. It was the same sentiment that drew her earlier.

Kali filled with hope. His hate would make her strong if she could get this man on her side. She slid her fingers through the darkness, willing a hole to appear. She felt the warmth of the real world caress her fingers. She followed her hand into the world, staying invisible so she could observe until she felt the time was right.

A tall man stood in front of a wide window watching something in the trees outside. They were in a house. The window opened onto a forest, trees filtering the light into a very pale green. It was soothing. Kali didn't want to be soothed. It made her angry and anger gave her strength.

The man was heavily built. His hair was cut long around his ears, iron grey, and lank it made him look older and tired. His soul would not provide her any energy even if he died screaming.

She looked on the desk that stood between her and the man. A book sat in the middle of it. This was a book of power, and not the kind she sought. The man was stiff with his own fury. She could see that the emotion was tainted with fear. He feared what was happening. That would work. But if he feared the glow, he would fear her. She had no leverage in her current form — yet.

Kali looked around the room. There were pictures of a man nailed to a cross, statues of gentle and insipid looking women. Causing her image to appear as one of the statues was like managing a puppet.

"You fear this change is not from your god," she said in a soft voice.

The man spun around. He was fair, his eyes grey and watery, his cheeks blared red. "How did you get into this room?"

Kali cast her eyes on the ground like the statues. "I was sent to help you. I was sent to warn you."

The man leaned on the desk as though he couldn't hold up his body otherwise. Kali wondered if he would be capable of what she needed.

"Who are you?" His voice was wary.

She sent her essence into his mind for the answer. Learning everything about him before a second had passed, she said, "An angel. I was sent to warn you about the evil that is stalking the world, and to support you in your righteous fight to save those souls that can be. This is the battle for good or evil. Are you ready?"

Her words straightened his back and put fire into his eyes. Kali smiled, but kept it inside, sure that the image she had chosen would not show pleasure at his reaction.

Patience was hard.

Hunger was pulling at her and he was taking so long to answer. She needed him to say the words, and then he would be hers.

"If my Lord wishes me to be his general then I am ready."

Kali made her image look up and then give a tiny smile. "Jeremiah Nielson, you are exactly what is needed."

The use of his name was like turning on a light. It was like proof to him. Kali felt the hunger for power radiate from him as much as she felt the pull of her own hunger.

"What do we need to do?" Jeremiah asked.

The need to feed was too strong for Kali to stay. She could feel herself slipping through to the darkness again. "I cannot remain here, but I will return when God sends me again. It will be soon, very soon."

She let the image fade before slipping back into the darkness, chasing the sound of pain and horror.

THE FEELING OF UNCERTAINTY WAS STRANGE TO TRAHAEARN. Used to knowing exactly what to do, asking for help in this critical situation was uncomfortable — no, it was damn annoying. He left Dionne in the kitchen putting together sandwiches while he thought. He'd have to ask her to help. She might be little more than a child, but humans raised her as a human, so she would have insights into that world. He could trust her more than he could bring himself to trust Jacob.

He needed to walk, and usually he would go out and pace the circle of trees. That wasn't an option now. If two humans had breached the defense, there could be more people on their way. The museum was big enough to let him burn off some frustration with physical effort. He ran up the stairs to the top floor.

This area had escaped the notice of the vampires. The rows of books seemed to call to him, their knowledge thirsting for him as much as he thirsted for theirs. Even through the thick layer of dust the books were in good condition. He would have his druids spend time cleaning here as therapy. He circled the floor letting the calm of the library leach his frustrations and let him find peace.

A few circuits of the floor and he was weary of the repetition, returning downstairs, Trahaearn looked around. The main floor was still in a mess. He walked through the offices and lab where he'd managed to clear the debris but it needed a good cleaning, and then the equipment would have to be replaced. The practical thoughts were as soothing as the knowledge held in the books upstairs. He'd speak to Gareth about creating an inventory of what they needed. Perhaps a couple of others would heal enough to start working in a few days. And Dionne, if she had to do magic, would be able to burn off the glow with some hard physical work. That was really their only safety net, at least until the humans were comfortable enough with magic to make it safe to glow in public.

Below him were two levels of basement with living quarters and storage, and then another final level where they call the circle. In fact, he would have Dionne set the circle now. Jacob had promised to call as soon as he had arranged a time to meet with the two politicians. He was confident that Jacob knew how urgent it was, that the longer it took to get moving forward, the more likely it would be that violence would erupt.

"YOU WANT TO JUST CALL THEM?" DIONNE SAID AS SHE CLOSED the containment circle "Will Maeve be okay with a summons?"

Trahaearn knew it wouldn't normally be okay to summon anyone. "Be polite, ask them to come, tell them we have information."

She rolled her eyes. Did he have to give her permission to speak? That was odd since she'd seemed overly willing to offer her opinion before the prophecy happened. Perhaps she was feeling guilty over her role in the change that the prophecy had wrought. "You have something to say?"

Dionne shrugged. "I'm not sure they need to be brought up to date with every step. I think they expect you to tell them when something is done, and that won't be until we've met with these two people."

Surprised at her wisdom, he said, "You are probably right. There are two reasons we're calling them. One is to make sure your assumption is the right one, and the other reason is that I want to make sure they will come when we need them."

She smiled and gave him a nod. The Arch Druid didn't need the approval of a young witch, but the man in Trahaearn felt glad she approved.

The other three came to the circle within a few minutes of Dionne's call.

"What do you need from us, druid?" Maeve asked, the others letting her take the lead.

Trahaearn waited a beat before answering. It was critical for him to know they would trust him. It was fine for them to say that they did, but things would happen rapidly when it started, and he wouldn't have time to stop and confer. "We have made some progress. We've made a contact who will help. Do you want to know who he is?"

Maeve waved her hand elegantly. "I trust you. You only need to contact me when you require me to do something. Or, I suppose, to warn me about something." Her image blinked out.

"I agree with Maeve," Mark rumbled before flicking out.

"Well, that's you told," Beacon said on a chuckle. "I trust you Trahaearn. I have no agenda but to keep my people safe. I will give you what support you need. It may not be much, but when you need a fairy, or sprite, or any other creature under my protection, I will find a way to make it happen. We are all willing to risk our lives to save the Real Folk." Beacon's image faded away.

Trahaearn motioned for Dionne to break the circle. He didn't like using her for all the magic, but he couldn't risk being aglow when he met these politicians.

She was improving. A massacre somewhere fed Kali enough to let her ignore the hunger without fading. But she still burned the energy almost as fast as she drank it. When she was strong, she would learn more about this world, but for now, she simply flowed to the greatest pain. When she was strong, that pain would be throughout the world.

Returning to Jeremiah Nielson's study, Kali found him in the same position she had left him. Was she able to travel through time, or did her feeding take no time? It would be good to investigate when she had the energy. All that mattered now was creating chaos to send more souls along to the next plane, so she would be strong enough to learn about the world.

"I have returned," she said as she formed the vision of the penitent. Jeremiah's mind had provided all the information she needed to convince him to do her bidding; facts furred with emotion and greed and intent. All she cared for were the facts. He would supply all of the rest.

"You have more information?" he asked.

Kali nodded. "This glow is an affliction of the devil. Those who glow are doing the devil's work. You must bring the people back to God's way no matter what it takes."

He smiled, a thin and joyless expression. "Increasing my flock will make me powerful. I can lead the whole area to God."

She didn't care what he did as long as there were deaths. "The whole world, perhaps?"

"How do I contact their leaders? I need to find them and save them." He was glowing with religious fever, something only Kali could see.

"You will find them in the forest. They will be hard to approach, but they are there."

A gleam of some emotion Kali couldn't identify brought life to his eyes. "This will convince the other religious leaders to heed my advice. I will bring these devil's agents to the light."

That was not necessarily going to give her power. "The devil is inside them. You will have to drive it out. You will have to purge the evil."

"That is exactly what we will do." Jeremiah turned to the window again. "Look out there." He gestured to the trees. "The devil will not take this beauty from me."

Kali grinned behind the image of piety. The man was hers.

He turned to look at her again. "Which forest? This one?"

She caused her image to drop her gaze. "They are collected in the forest park. The one in the city. Others are near there, but you must start with the ones in the forest."

"Stanley Park. There have been sightings. I will call my congregation to act. We can be ready within days." Jeremiah reached for his phone.

Kali was hungry again. If the man could act faster, it would be better, but she needed to go and find more pain to feed upon. "As soon as you can. God will reward you for acting with speed."

Jeremiah smiled again, this time there was ambition and greed echoing in his soul.

Kali left him to his preparations. She needed to feed, and then learn what the druid was doing to foil her.

6

Trahaearn waited in the hall for Jacob to knock. Dionne had cleared out one of the smaller rooms on the main floor for the meeting. The physical work had diminished her glow enough so she could sit at the table and seem human. When she did magic, the glow would be stronger, and it would be clear that it was the result of the magic. Gareth was guarding the doorway to the infirmary to keep the other druids away.

It had been a long day. As much as he wanted to rest, Trahaearn was pleased that things were moving fast. If things continued to go this well, he'd be working on a plan to manage Kali by the end of the week.

A rap on the door interrupted his thoughts. It was time for the show to start.

Trahaearn opened the door to find Jacob standing on the top step with two people behind him. A woman dressed in a bright green sari and a lot of gold jewelry, all of which clashed with the briefcase she carried. The other was a man wearing a dark blue business suit and a curious look.

Jacob stepped forward when Trahaearn motioned for him to

enter. "This is Angela Singh and Glen Watson. They are city council members who are interested in understanding what is going on."

"We have a room where we can meet in private," Trahaearn said, leading the way after shaking the proffered hands. "Has Jacob told you anything?"

Angela smiled and shook her head. "He was very mysterious, but he assured us that we were in no danger meeting you here, brother? Is that the right term?"

"Trahaearn. No other title is needed."

"You are going to explain what this glowing is about?" Glen said in a tone that showed he was used to being in charge.

Trahaearn nodded and opened the meeting room door. "When we are inside. I will tell you and show you." He hoped that they would be as easily convinced as Jacob, but below Angela's politeness and Glen's take charge attitude, there was a suspicion that wasn't present in Jacob's personality. It was a talent Jacob would have to cultivate if he was going to be successful in journalism.

Dionne looked up from the table as they came in. She smiled as though long-lost friends had entered. "Good evening. Can I get you some tea? Coffee? Water. I'm afraid we have nothing stronger."

Jacob shook his head and settled into one of the chairs.

"Perhaps later. We are anxious to hear the story," Angela said and then took her seat.

Trahaearn watched Glen react to Dionne. The girl was beautiful. Her long blond hair and fair skin marking her as having sidhe blood. It was a look of innocence and allure. Something about her seemed to affect Glen more than just seeing a beautiful woman. He seemed afraid somehow. Perhaps his subconscious had identified her beauty as non-human.

He took control of his reaction fast, which made Trahaearn wonder if he'd been mistaken.

Glen pulled out his chair. "I will also wait until we are finished our business. I don't have all day, so perhaps we can begin?"

Trahaearn nodded and sat. "What I have to tell you might be difficult for you to accept. Would you allow me to first tell you why it has happened?"

He waited until they agreed before starting to speak. "There was a prophecy. One that everyone involved expected to come about eventually. It was known for centuries. Everyone had begun to think it would always be in the far future, but in the last year, all of the aspects came together. The signs were clear that the prophecy would come to pass, but there was no indication of what would happen." He paused.

"Is this a religious prophecy? Perhaps you should be speaking to a reverend, or rabbi, or perhaps an imam?" Glen suggested.

At least he was participating in the conversation. Angela simply waited for Trahaearn to continue.

"No, I believe Jacob was right in bringing you here. The prophecy occurred, and now we are dealing with the fallout. I know we cannot keep this secret for much longer, but I worry that if we do not manage the message, so to speak, it will cause terrible damage. Would you be willing to take an oath that you will not use the information to cause harm?"

Glen's eyes narrowed, but it was Angela who answered, "No, we have an obligation to our constituents. I will assure you that, despite the comments from our opponents, I am not in the habit of doing harm, neither is Mr. Watson. Please tell us what you need to say, and we will think on what we can do to help, or at least, contain the problem."

He took a deep breath pushing his suspicions of the humans aside so he could reveal what they needed to know.

"There are people who exist beside you in this world who have, until a few days ago, been invisible to you."

Glen started to rise. "Please. If you are going to tell us a fairy-tale, I have more important things to do with my time."

"Glen, for heaven's sake," Jacob said reaching to touch the man's elbow. "I promise this is going to be more important than anything you have scheduled."

"I don't know you well, Mr. Myers, but my people tell me you are reliable." Glen turned to look at Trahaearn. "Go on, but make it quick."

Trahaearn swallowed the urge to smack the man down for his insolence. No one spoke to the Arch Druid in that manner, but the humans didn't know how to behave, and patience was probably more useful right now than power. He continued as if Glen hadn't interrupted. "They are the people of mythology. Yes, they are fairies, and sprites, and imps, and witches and wizards and others. These people are magic and can perform magic. They mean no harm to humans, but since the prophecy we have glowed. We fear the harm you may do to us."

He watched their reaction. Jacob and Dionne were doing the same.

Angela looked at Trahaearn, seeming to seek for truth or trick. Glen seemed angry and his mouth moved as though he was trying to put together words that would convince everyone they were wrong. Trahaearn's anger was under control, and he wasn't afraid of the man's reaction. It was honest, and it gave him some idea of the starting point. Trahaearn waited it out. One of them would speak at some point. When that happened, he would ask Dionne to demonstrate.

Glen broke the silence. "I do not believe this story. It is ridiculous. If you don't know the answer to this mysterious phenomenon say so. Please do not waste our time."

He didn't move to leave, so Trahaearn was sure the words were simply bluster.

Angela seemed more curious than afraid. "I see that you have convinced Jacob. He is not an idiot, but he is idealistic. I imagine you provided some proof? Will you do so with us?"

Before Trahaearn could agree, Glen spoke again, "Yes, produce a fairy for us to marvel over."

"I will, eventually, introduce you to some of the other beings, but the fairies are hiding, and they are afraid of humans. Dionne will provide proof. She is a witch. I am a druid — the Arch Druid for this part of the world. Dionne?"

She stood and smiled. "I can do this," she said, then levitated and invited Angela and Glen to verify that there were no supports beneath or around her. When they were done, she said, "And this." She waved her hands and the room filled with butterflies.

Trahaearn was pleased she'd moved on from bees.

When it was clear that the butterflies were real, she made them disappear, and then she cast a glamor on herself, changing from a beautiful young girl, to a troll, to a kobold, and then back to herself. "That's a little sample of the type of people you will eventually see. Is there anything else you would like me to demonstrate?"

They didn't answer because they were staring at her glow; the spells had caused a bright amber shine to appear on Dionne's exposed skin.

Dionne raised her arms. "Oh, yes. This is what happens when any of us do magic."

It took a moment for Angela to react. She reached to touch Dionne, stopping to ask permission before she placed her hand on the glowing arm. Glen moved backward, only a little, but it worried Trahaearn. If he were afraid, or repelled by what he'd seen, there would be trouble. He needed both of these politicians on his side. If he only had Angela, he would be facing all of her opponents. Regardless of their private views, they would attack. With Glen on their side, there were fewer opponents. Jacob must have chosen these two for a reason. He wanted the story of a life-time, of an era, and he wouldn't risk it by bringing in people he didn't trust to help.

When it seemed they'd absorbed the information a little,

Trahaearn said, "You must be in shock, but I need to know if you are willing to help us."

Glen answered first. "By help what do you want? I will not help you take over. I will not help you use this power for... well, not for things I oppose."

Trahaearn looked at Angela who had finished her inspection of Dionne's skin. "I assume you are not going to do anything that we would consider a threat. If I am understanding correctly, you, all of you, have lived among us for as long as we have been here. If you wanted to control us, you would already be doing so."

Dionne regained her seat, rubbing at her skin as though it burned. Trahaearn raised an eyebrow but she shook her head, as though to say, 'you are on your own for that one'.

Trahaearn decided that the truth was his best option. "I can guarantee that humans would eventually find a way to get out from any power we could wield. In fact, when humans and Real Folk clashed in the past, Real Folk died, not humans."

"How are you so sure what the humans will do?" Glen asked.

Trahaearn let Dionne answer so that he could try to work out the man's real problem. He was acting angry, but he wasn't radiating any strong emotion. There was some fear, but not enough to concern anyone. Angela was also a little afraid. Perhaps that's how humans reacted to such news. To be honest, he wondered if humans had suddenly appeared to Real Folk, would the reaction have been any different?

"I was raised as a human," Dionne said. "I always felt like I didn't quite fit. But I didn't know who I was until a few months ago. My parents were killed to try to stop the prophecy, but it couldn't be stopped." Tears shone in her eyes. Dionne wiped them away with her arm and gave a shaky smile.

Trahaearn had forgotten how raw the loss of her parents was to Dionne. It had happened when she was an infant, but she'd only learned the significance recently.

Angela patted Dionne in sympathy. "I am sorry to hear that

your parents died." Then she turned to Glen. "I think we need to be part of this. If we can help stop what could be a massacre, we are obligated to do so."

"I am not sure we are picking the right side," he said. Leaning his elbows on the table, he steepled his hands and touched his chin almost professorial in attitude. The fear was driven away to Trahaearn's relief. "What is it that you want us to do?" Glen asked.

Jacob had been silent the entire time. He'd taken notes, and grinned at Dionne's demonstration — probably relieved it wasn't bees — but he was clearly not willing to influence events. Trahaearn didn't want him to be just an observer. If Jacob became involved, his reporting would have more passion, and they needed that.

Before he revealed how little planning they had done, Trahaearn needed to know about the humans who would be his allies. "What did Jacob tell you?"

Jacob looked up from his notes. "I didn't tell them anything more than that they would have a chance to be involved in resolving the crisis that was building over the glow. I did say you needed them, but not why."

Glen leaned in and said, "I sense that you have no plan. How could you when you didn't know who we were, and how we might help?"

Nodding, Trahaearn answered, "We have an agreement amongst the Real Folk. There are a few of us who will negotiate with the humans. I have been given the authority to work with you until we are sure it is safe. I don't have much of a plan, but I do know what we want. There must be harmony eventually, but for now, we need to live together without fear, or violence. We only have so much time to accomplish that."

Glancing at Angela before speaking, Glen said, "No one wants to see things come to violent ends. If we bring our constituents to this, you will have to speak to them. Are you prepared to use this magic to convince everyone as you did with us?"

"If needed, but is there any expectation that we can keep it secret after one demonstration?"

Glen looked to Angela again, but this time she spoke, "We must be careful how we release the news. Jacob here can manage the message. It is important that people believe, but I think it is more important that they do not panic."

"I think a televised press conference," Jacob said. "We get the most coverage and we control the message — and the images. At least until they hit the internet and people alter them."

"We want to be on stage with you," Glen stated. "We want to be seen as your allies." He looked around and added, "It will allow us to support you better. If we are there, we do not have to justify our help later. It will solidify us as the leaders of this new cause."

Trahaearn didn't like the avarice in Glen's tone but couldn't argue. They needed to portray a solid team, not seem to be jumping on bandwagons. "When? And how will we use this to save our people?" he asked.

Angela stood. "Jacob will work with you for that. I will start reaching out to my contacts. We need them primed to join us as soon as they hear. Glen will do the same." She waited for him to nod. "I trust you have some way to manage the international approach?"

That would be good, he thought, but he had to be honest with them. "This is the most populated area for Real Folk. The others are in hiding — so far mostly successful. From the Real Folk we have consensus that they will abide with the agreements we make here. I am hoping the humans over the world will agree too. If not, we will see an influx of new Real Folk as they escape whatever evils are visited on them."

Angela picked up her briefcase. "We can't solve all the problems at once. When will we meet others of your kind?"

Trahaearn wanted to prepare first and ask that some of the others attend the circle. "Will you come back here? I can summon people to a circle. You will see their images, and you can ask them questions."

Glen answered, "I do not wish to participate in any magical ritual. I hope I don't offend with that. I will meet someone, or several someones, face to face if you can arrange it."

Trahaearn looked to Angela, she simply looked back, giving him no support for any argument he might muster. "I can take you to the forest. I will need to take some precautions. Will you agree to a blindfold?" He wouldn't lead them to the location of the forest Real Folk, but that would be the best place to meet a variety of magical folk, people who *were* magic rather than simply did magic. He was sure he could get Beacon to agree.

Glen nodded, and Angela said, "Tonight? In two hours? We can meet at the entrance on Nicola Street to be more discreet. I will not bring anyone. Glen do you feel the same?"

Trahaearn could see that Glen didn't want to say yes in the way his eyes shifted to the door. The man was now truly afraid. Trahaearn couldn't help him with a magical nudge. He would have to come to his own terms in the pull between his need for the exposure and his fear.

"I will come alone," he said, reluctantly. "I do not like the idea of being blindfolded, but I understand the need for caution. But Jacob may not attend. No press."

ngela was there early and eager. They were waiting for Glen, and Trahaearn could feel the tension building with every minute that passed. He'd spent time convincing Beacon and Maeve that this was needed, and that they should attend. Beacon had been easy to convince of the need, but he refused to allow Trahaearn to bring humans to the hiding places. He'd suggested a small clearing just inside the trees near the entrance to the park. The glow would be hidden, and it was far enough away from the real sanctuary to ensure safety. And it meant they didn't need to be blindfolded.

Dionne was still acting as Trahaearn's assistant. Lionel had stayed at the museum looking for any information on Kali.

"I'll call him again," Angela said. Glen's lateness was annoying her.

Trahaearn could see the shine of anticipation in her eyes. She was like a child before a birthday party, looking for reasons to get her present sooner.

"No need, I'm here," Glen announced as he stepped from a taxi. "I had a meeting. It felt more important today to attend and keep my influence active by seeming normal, than it was to arrive on time."

Angela looked at her watch. "Fine, it's already after eight pm and we still need to find this clearing."

Trahaearn informed them that the blindfolds would not be required and led them into the park. As they walked toward the denser stand of trees farther in, Angela chattered, seeming unable to contain her curiosity. She had clearly been in charge before, but now it was Glen taking a power position. He was silent; her chatter causing him to clench his teeth.

"I spent some time reviewing your western mythology before I came," Angela said. "You mentioned fairies, will there be one at this meeting?"

Trahaearn motioned for Dionne to take the lead. "Yes, Queen Bud of the rose fairies will attend. I would ask that you remember she leads one of the largest clans, despite her size and childlike appearance. She will expect to be treated as a leader."

"Yes, of course. Now, what about vampires," Angela asked. "They are very popular at the moment in entertainment. I confess I do not look forward to meeting any creature who survives by drinking blood." She turned her attention to the path, stepping carefully to avoid tripping.

Vampires were a delicate subject. Trahaearn still hadn't fully dealt with the feelings he had about what they had done. "There are no vampires left." He wanted to leave it at that, but his teaching habits were too strong. "They didn't live off blood, they lived off the life force of companions. They did not need much and most formed strong relationships so they could feed on willing subjects."

Dionne looked at him over her shoulder, surprise on her face. When they got through the worst of this crisis, he would need to assess what gaps she had in her knowledge.

"Why are there only western magical folk?" Glen asked,

before Angela could speak again. It was as if he wanted his fair share of the conversation now that Trahaearn had joined in.

"There are some non-western beings. We have a family of nymphs who are native to China, but for some reason most other magical creatures chose to remain closer to home. Perhaps that will change when we have agreed on our coexistence."

Glen gave a rare smile. "I'm not sure the world is ready for real dragons to appear, or genies."

Angela looked at him surprised at the humor. "My culture also has some rather violent beings. We mostly think of gods when we think of magic."

The thought of dealing with gods didn't appeal to Trahaearn. One Kali was enough. "You will meet several people tonight. Maeve will attend, she is the Queen of sidhe, and Beacon who is a sprite and leads all of the Real Folk in the park. I've asked if they will invite Olan. He's a pixie and very independent. There are others, but they cannot roam the streets undiscovered."

Dionne held up her hand to stop their progress. "We'll be there in a moment. Please don't take offense to anything that might be said. These people have had good reason to fear humans, and they are really proud."

Angela looked to Glen, asserting her leadership again. "We will treat everyone with respect, and we will not take offense easily. I hope we will be treated with the same consideration."

Dionne nodded, but Trahaearn could see she wasn't convinced. "I will introduce you as leaders of your communities," she said. "That should make your status clear. Are you ready?"

They stepped between the last trees to enter a glade. Dionne's witch light formed a dome of illumination, and an empty clearing. Trahaearn was the last one through, which put him in the best position to stop Glen from leaving. Far from having a thick skin, the man was already muttering angrily because they were the first to arrive.

Trahaearn blocked the way to avoid having Glen slip past in

annoyance. "They will be here when we have settled. When everyone has arrived, Dionne will cast a spell that will keep people away — both human and Real Folk. Please find a comfortable place to sit."

The clearing was carpeted with old leaves and fallen pine needles. They each found a place to sit, the humans together, druid and witch across from them.

As the little sounds of the forest returned, a soft warm voice said, "Dionne, please douse the light."

Beacon, at least, had come.

Dionne closed her hand and the clearing went dark, illuminated only by the glow produced by her magic. Then a bright flicker approached. Queen Bud settled on Trahaearn's shoulder. A larger, slower moving green aura announced Beacon's approach. Even at more than ten feet tall, he made no sound.

When he entered the clearing, Beacon rested against a tree, turned to look behind him and gave a sigh. "Olan, come on. It's not like you to hang back. Aren't you supposed to be the great protector of the humans?"

Olan strode into the clearing. Tiny, dressed in a scrap of lilac velvet and carrying a bobbin decorated with feathers, he grumbled, "That doesn't mean I want to hang out with them." He sat between Trahaearn and Angela. "Where is Maeve? We need to get this started."

Trahaearn knew exactly where the sidhe queen was standing. Maeve was not glowing like the others. She waited just at the edge of the clearing, where his party had entered. At the sound of her name, Maeve flicked her fingers and a regal chair appeared, the glow that accompanied it was sapphire blue and strong.

Ignoring Maeve's theatrics, Trahaearn said, "Dionne, seal us in, please."

Trahaearn watched as people recovered from the shock. The Real Folk, as much as they tried to appear powerful, radiated fear and distrust for anyone who could read the small signs. The tightening of Maeve's usually smooth brow, Bud's constant fidgeting, Olan's casual appraisal of his bobbin, and Beacon's tense pose, were all indications of distress. Even Trahaearn was feeling the crawling of imaginary insects across his shoulders. No one wanted to be here, but they all knew that it was unavoidable if they wanted their species to survive.

He made the introductions and everyone behaved graciously. Now it was time to start the real talks, the ones that would eventually lead to harmony.

"Before we go further, does anyone have any questions that need to be answered? Anything that will make you more comfortable?" he asked.

Bud flew off his shoulder and circled the humans. Their heads moved around with her flight. It wasn't clear if that was due to fascination, or terror, or perhaps a little of both.

"Are you planning to kill us and eat us?" Bud asked.

Angela, to her credit, took the question seriously. "No. We are here to plan peace. Is it your intention to enchant us into your slaves?"

A peal of wicked laughter filled the clearing. Bud moved closer to Angela, hand raised as though to cast a spell. Instead, she darted in and kissed Angela's brow. "No. I like you." She flew back to Dionne. "That is a nice human. I am not so afraid now."

Trust Bud to break the tension.

Trahaearn looked to Maeve. The fairies and the sidhe had a long-established hatred for each other, even though they were related. Maeve simply looked amused. He decided to take it at face value. The internal problems of the Real Folk could stay under the veneer of politeness until relationships were settled with the humans.

"We came together in person for a reason," Beacon said. "What do you want, humans?"

Glen bristled at the tone.

Beacon was usually all helpfulness and kindness. This hard

attitude must come from fear. Trahaearn intervened before they could get into an ego fight. "I believe Angela and Glen are here to understand that we are truly real. And that not all of us can pass for human."

"Do you have any questions of us?" Angela asked.

Olan stepped into the center of the circle. "We just want to know if you are planning to slaughter us. If that answer is yes, we'll have to get ready to fight, if not, then let's get on with it."

The two humans exchanged glances. Olan could be a mighty force regardless of his size. Glen finally nodded to Angela. She stood and looked down on Olan. Trahaearn readied himself. If Angela thought she could intimidate Olan, she was going to be in for a shock.

She didn't try to speak down to him. Trahaearn realized she was doing her best to mimic Olan's stance to make him comfortable. "We are going to do everything we can to prevent deaths on either side. Can you speak for every individual of your kind? Why did the large one call you the protector of humans?"

"It's a long story," Olan huffed.

Trahaearn raised an eyebrow. He hadn't heard the tale and it must be embarrassing given the pixie's attitude. "We have time for you to tell it. We are here to make allies, after all."

Olan sat on the ground. "I'll shorten it. I made a mistake a long time ago. It's not really important what the mistake was, but Raven caught me and punished me."

"Raven?" Glen asked. "The Haida Raven?" He seemed to notice the surprise on everyone's face. "I'm on the First Nations committee. I did some research."

Olan played with the feathers on his bobbin, like a small child fidgeting to avoid being scolded. "Yes, that Raven. Well he thought it would be a fine joke to make me responsible for protecting the humans. It's been a chore, but I've saved your lives more than once since."

The acknowledgement that the First Nations mythology was

alive and well seemed to lift a weight from both of the humans. Trahaearn guessed there was a political problem attached to the idea. "They have retired to another plane. It doesn't mean they won't be back, but my understanding is that no one has seen Raven, or Bear, or any of the others in centuries."

Olan looked at the ground. "Not my fault."

"I hardly think a pixie has the power to send the old ones away, even one as charming and powerful as you, Olan." Maeve's words were softened by a chuckle. "Do you need to hear all of our history? It will take longer than we have."

Angela shook her head. "For me, I am convinced that you exist, and that others exist that we don't yet know. I am curious, but perhaps that can wait until later. We should speak about what you are willing to let Trahaearn say in the press release we are issuing."

Beacon pulled away from the tree he was leaning against. "I think it best you tell humans what we bring as value to their lives. That's what my folk overhear all the time from families in the park. Humans are only interested in what will benefit them."

Trahaearn looked to Dionne. She had flushed but didn't argue. Beacon was probably right about most humans — and Real Folk. "That's a good idea. In fact, we can start with the forest folk, it's the most clear benefit."

Glen shifted his position, preparing to rise. "What is that benefit?"

Trahaearn waited until the man was standing before answering, "The sprites, fairies, and nymphs all benefit the living plants. Fairies in your garden mean your flowers are more beautiful, your herbs more potent, and your vegetables more abundant. Without the sprites and nymphs, this park would die."

Something gleamed in Glen's eye. "So, these folk would be a benefit to agriculture?"

Beacon spoke before Trahaearn could answer. "Only if they are free. Do not think to enslave the forest folk to your ends. It's time for us to return, Bud, Olan, I'm going."

When it was just Maeve left with them, Angela asked, "And the sidhe? What can we say about the benefit you will bring?"

Trahaearn waited along with the humans. What would Maeve say? 'I'm a better politician than any of your leaders' or 'my people are more beautiful than any of your celebrities.'

When she spoke, it was both a surprise and expected. "We shall see what that is as we build the peace between our peoples. For now, I suggest you stay focused on the forest folk." She rose, flicked a hand to make the chair disappear and then glided out of the clearing.

8

T he next morning, Trahaearn waited for the humans to settle in the meeting room. Dionne was working with Lionel to clear the main floor of the damage done in the battle with the vampires. Trahaearn knew that at some point, people would want to come to the museum, and it had to look like a place of study, not the aftermath of a biker gang war.

It wasn't comfortable being alone with the humans, but Trahaearn knew that they would take it as a sign of trust if he didn't need to surround himself with Real Folk. When they were all settled in, with tea and muffins to fortify them, Trahaearn said, "It makes sense to me to allow Jacob to lead us here. I believe he has the knowledge we need."

Jacob looked up from his notes, surprised. "I'm not the public relations expert. Maybe Angela or Glen?"

Glen shook his head. "We just follow the advice of our PR person when it comes to announcements. The mayor will have to know of course. He may want to make the announcement."

Panic flitted across Jacob's face then cleared. "I know someone who could help."

"No one else can be involved," Trahaearn commanded. "The more people, the more the risk of our message not being ours."

"Okay, okay, give me a second." Jacob pulled out his phone. "I can call this person and get advice without giving anything away. Would that work?"

Trahaearn looked to Angela and Glen. They nodded. "Do not tell this person where you are," he said.

To Trahaearn it seemed that Jacob was careful to provide enough information without giving specifics. He ended the call sounding more confident, and then stood looking at the notes he'd made.

"I swear she can be trusted," he said. When no one agreed to bring the woman into the group, he continued, "You have to look like you aren't a threat. So, Trahaearn, the tattoos have to be hidden. You should have Dionne there too. She's young and pretty and human looking. You have to give the facts and keep to the message that your people are here to help us. Don't mention anything that could seem like you are powerful. Don't answer questions about magic controlling humans, or anything bad."

Trahaearn knew he could get Dionne ready, but would it not be odd to only answer questions they liked. "What do we do with those questions we are not willing to answer? I don't think we can ignore them."

Glen and Angela both laughed. Glen said, "You just turn it around to what you need to say. If they ask you, 'aren't you really just planning to control us with magic?' you say 'Magic is used to help, and in peace we can help the most.' Just keep your answers to the key message. You want to help. You can help."

It wasn't that different from arguing within the grove. What was going to be different were the cameras, and that any slip could go out to the world. Trahaearn was tired of the delays. "When? Can we do it today?"

Jacob shrugged. "Why not. Let's agree on the message, and I'll get the press ready. We can do it outside the museum. It's a calm place and a testament to the power being healthy and peaceful."

"I'll ask Dionne to join us. I think we Real Folk will need to practice." Trahaearn went to the door and called for her.

"One more thing," Jacob said. "Calling yourselves Real Folk could suggest we humans aren't real. Could we call you something like Magical Folk?"

"We don't call ourselves Real Folk; we are Real Folk," Trahaearn said. Hearing the defensiveness in his voice, he added, "Perhaps we can avoid using the term Real Folk. You see how I am learning?"

Jacob laughed as he gathered his notes and left.

KALI STARED THROUGH THE VEIL AT THE GROUP IN THE MUSEUM room. That druid was undermining her authority on this world. His friends stank of cooperation. It weakened her just by existing. She needed to act.

It would be easier if all the humans could see her, or any of them other than Jeremiah. The effort of making herself visible was too much drain on her. When she was stronger, she would walk the earth, her very image causing terror and death. She would be unstoppable.

For now, it was enough to plant ideas in the minds of the humans who were willing to cause trouble. Not all humans were ready, but more than a few were eager to serve her, even if they didn't know who she was.

Kali drew back from the room to see what was happening in the surrounding area. The trees were doing a good job of confusing anyone who wandered toward the clearing. Only someone determined to get through would make it. If she had a great deal of luck, humans would soon see what she could: the glow of the magic that infused these trees. Then they would come looking for the threat and create the havoc she needed.

Stretching her senses to the limit, Kali saw that there were many people outside the trees seeking an outlet for their anger. She reached out a finger to touch the head of one such man. The henna pattern on the back of her hand pulsed as she made contact, turning from the traditional brown to a deep red.

The man's mind was alert to suggestion. Kali told him that the source of everything unfair was located at the center of the trees.

The man came to a complete stop, looked to his right, and then marched through the first of the guardian trees to find justice for all the unfairness that the world laid on his life.

It took her only moments to find ten others to send. Then she watched people follow her new disciples. These were curious and would be the chaos that she needed to create. Not all of the followers were angry enough to please her. Those that were not angry enough had value too — they would make good sacrifices.

Kali continued to drive people to the museum, only stopping when she had a crowd large enough to do damage when they panicked. She smiled at the thought of the druid caught in a riot, trampled to death. He would give her great power, and his death would remove one more obstacle to her rule.

When she was sure there were enough people closing in on the druid's home, Kali returned through the veil to the clearing outside the druid museum. Not all of her puppets had made it to the center. Some had drifted off as soon as they were out of her sight, but there were fifty at least who had persevered through the distraction spells. It would be enough.

There was one more thing she needed to test. It would take more of her power than she should spare, but if she could be seen, then it would replenish quickly with the terror she generated. She focused on the trees just behind her disciples and forced her being from the universe of the veil to the human world. She knew she'd succeeded when she could feel the rough, dry trunk of the tree under her palm. The scent of crushed leaves and needles filled her lungs, and for a moment she felt the pleasure of life around her. Then she collapsed to the ground.

Had she given too much power to get here?

Familiar terror flooded out the sensations of a moment ago. Would she be able to get back? Then a new disciple wandered past her. One she hadn't commanded. Good. The crowd was attracting its own new members, which meant she wouldn't have to use her own energy. Still afraid that she was stuck in this world until there were deaths nearby, Kali stepped forward.

No one paid attention.

She moved to stand close to one of the newcomers. She should be gloriously obvious in this crowd of drably dressed humans. Where they wore rough plain clothes, she was dressed in brilliant silks with rubies and sapphires sewn in intricate patterns.

No one turned to look at her.

She stepped forward, now the humans behind would surely panic at the sight of the blue woman in their midst.

Nothing.

She reached out to touch the nearest human. Kali shivered as her hand passed through the body of the woman. The woman shuddered and grasped her chest, knees buckling. Power started to seep into Kali as the human collapsed, but it stopped as soon as they lost contact.

So, she couldn't be seen, but the expenditure of energy was not a failure. Kali could steal what she needed with just a touch. She shivered again at the thought of the destruction she could wield.

Suddenly tendrils of that power touched every part of her body, each with a slightly different taste. Humans rushed to the aid of the fallen woman. Kali could hear their voices echo in the ecstasy that vibrated within her from the life force of the crowd. A force that she sipped from as each person passed through her.

"What happened?"

"Who did this?"

"Move back. She needs air. Get away!"

The crowd was turning into a mob all by itself. Kali was losing focus as the power filled her.

"Someone in there must have done it."

Kali dragged her attention back to the humans. None of them seemed to miss the power she'd stolen. That was information she would think about later. Now, she had to give a little push, to turn this into a riot — to kill.

She reached out to the mind of the human who had spoken last, planted the words, and withdrew.

The man grabbed the closest human. "They did this. We need to get in there and stop it. We need to stop them from killing all of us."

A few of the crowd started to withdraw, but the others rushed to the doors of the museum. Two fell, trampled beneath the rush. Kali took their life force and used the power to return through the veil. A laugh of pure joy tore from her as she passed through. Looking back, she saw that some of the humans had heard her voice. Good, now she had real disciples.

TRAHAEARN STRODE TO THE DOOR. WHATEVER WAS GOING ON out there had taken a bad turn. He'd ordered everyone to stay hidden until he could find out what it was. The trees were no longer their defense. That meant he'd have to divert attention and energy away from preparing for the announcement to setting up an alert system. Perhaps Gareth could do that. It was critical that neither Trahaearn nor Dionne did magic until the announcement itself. The glow had to seem linked to the magic.

Dionne had tried to argue that she could help, but neither of the humans offered. Despite knowing it was what he'd asked, Trahaearn couldn't stop the thought that they were unwilling to commit by showing themselves to be aligned with him.

He shook off the suspicion. No matter the reason, they

needed to stay inside. He wouldn't endanger them by bringing them into what sounded like a riot.

He placed his hand on the door and used its magic to listen. He heard angry voices, and a scream, and then laughter that echoed as though it came from another world.

Opening the door, Trahaearn stared out over a crowd of humans who were surging toward him. He stood firm, counting on the magic of the door to keep them out.

"Stop," he said in the voice he used to command his grove.

The humans paused long enough to notice that he was there. Some at the edge drifted off, but there were some ringleaders still ready to push the mob forward.

It might take magic to calm them, but Trahaearn hoped he could still find someone who would listen to reason. "You are disturbing the peace of this place. What do you want?"

That slowed the crowd a little more. Trahaearn saw some of the mob look toward the humans he'd thought were driving the fury. He didn't wait for an answer. "You have injured some of your number." He pointed to the two people crumpled on the ground. The other humans had drawn away leaving a clear space. "Do you wish us to tend to them?" Offering help might just change the mood of enough of these humans to defuse the pending attack. He had little experience in calming violence. Druids did argue hotly over knowledge, but never to the level of battle.

"Who are you?" An angry voice called from the back of the crowd.

Why did humans always want to know that? As if knowing who someone said they were would solve all mysteries. He paused to consider what to answer. A lie now would undermine the message later today, but the truth now may cause more trouble. "Who I am is not important when people are injured." He pointed to the two fallen humans. They weren't moving and Trahaearn knew they were dead, but also knew that information might ignite the final fuse on this mob.

"It's your fault." The same voice answered. "Why are you here? Who are you?"

Before Trahaearn could find the words to avoid answering, five uniformed police officers entered the clearing. One spoke into what looked like a two-way radio microphone that was mounted on his shoulder.

Trahaearn watched the crowd become wary. If the police were competent, then the incident would be dealt with. If Kali had summoned these men, it would get out of hand again. He knew a calming spell would aid the police, but he also knew that if anyone became aware they had been bespelled, no amount of diplomacy would save Real Folk lives.

"What's going on here?" one officer asked. He was older than the others. His hand slid slightly closer to his weapon as he spoke. The others moved apart so that they formed a barrier.

Trahaearn answered quickly before any of the humans could speak. "These people are uninvited, officer. They are threatening me and my brothers."

The officer scanned the crowd and seemed to be considering the likelihood that arresting everyone would solve the problem. Before he took any action, something changed. Trahaearn felt a chill in his bones and then noticed a brilliant flicker behind the eyes of two of the angriest humans. Their expressions were frozen in rage, while everyone around them was becoming calmer as the police moved through the crowd. Something was using the two humans as puppets.

"He killed those two," one of the puppets shouted, pointing to the fallen humans.

The crowd separated so the officer had a clear view.

The other controlled human spoke, "We came to ask what was going on here. This building just appeared out of nowhere."

A crackle came from the radio. Trahaearn hoped they were calling for reinforcements. These five would have no chance if the two leaders were successful.

Knowing a straight denial would do nothing to clear the accusation, Trahaearn could only rely on reason. "I could not have done anything to them. Look where they are, in the middle of this crowd."

The cop signaled something to the other officers before stepping forward. "We got a call that there was a disturbance here. It seems that it was more than a simple disturbance. We'll need to let someone higher on the food chain sort this out. Everyone stay where you are." The officer kept moving forward, his pace steady.

Trahaearn watched carefully, trying to learn every nuance of the man's attitude. The crowd was, perhaps not calmed, but no longer being whipped up by the possessed humans. In the coming days, Trahaearn knew he'd need to be able to take control this way. No magic, just a subtle assumption of power.

The officer made it to the first downed human. He knelt and touched the wrist, confirming what everyone knew. Passing across to the other victim, he checked for a pulse and then rose. "Everyone needs to wait until we have your name, and your statement." He turned to look back at the other officers. "Call for back up and get a detective here. No one leaves until we give the okay."

"No. They did this," one of the two human puppets shouted. The other moved toward the officer, fists tight at his side.

The humans around them started to mutter. A laugh that only Trahaearn seemed to hear rode over the noise. Trahaearn knew that laugh.

Kali was driving these people to violence. If he were right, the authority of a few police would not stop the humans. If their reinforcements didn't arrive now, the riot would start again. He stepped outside and reached behind him to close the door to the museum. If their efforts failed, at least the rioters wouldn't have easy access to those within.

The other officers started to move toward the crowd. Trahaearn saw some of the mob drift off into the trees, unwilling to stay and become part of the growing madness. It gave him hope that some of the humans could resist Kali's influence.

IT WASN'T WORKING. SOMEHOW THE DRUID HAD INTERFERED. The ones she had chosen to speak with her words were not strong enough. These humans in uniform had brought with them a calming influence that allowed the mob to stop when there were only two bodies.

Kali watched closely, not having the energy to take over any more of the humans. The quiet moans and whimpers of the injured didn't produce the energy she needed to replenish her strength. The two bodies would have to do.

The next time she would have more information and would have more deaths to feed upon. The uniformed humans were hesitating, but not enough for Kali to act. One of them called for help. Some of her own humans skulked off into the trees. She could sense others passing, one coming toward the circle.

"No. We told you. They did this," one of her disciples shouted.

Hope filled Kali as the remaining crowd started to move in on the uniformed humans. Trahaearn had no chance to stop this. He was alone. The others she could sense inside the building were not coming to his aid.

"You need to take a step back, sir," the older uniformed human said. His words were polite, his tone commanding.

"We want justice for our fallen," the disciple shouted. "Arrest this man."

The crowd started chanting 'arrest him' and the uniformed human reached for the weapon on his hip.

This just lit a fire under Kali's followers. They started to surge forward, but something held them back from actually attacking.

"On your knees," the uniformed human shouted. There was a tinge of panic in the sound, but Kali realized the other humans hadn't heard it.

Kali pushed as hard as she dared, but years of conditioning stood in her way. The disciples were not listening. They stopped and waited. Not dropping to their knees, but still more compliant than she wanted. The longer they waited the weaker her hold on them became.

The uniformed human waved to the others. "We need to figure out what happened. Start taking statements. You," he called to the druid. "Don't go anywhere."

"I think I'm supposed to tell you I'm filming." A new voice came from the edge of the trees.

The humans on the rim of the crowd turned to look. The uniformed humans kept their attention on the crowd. The druid remained calm and solid, standing as if guarding the building.

Kali spat her anger at the world she was too weak to enter.

"Who are you?" the human in charge asked.

"Name's Jacob Myers. I'm here with the press." He held up his small tablet where Kali saw moving pictures. "One tap and it's streaming out to the world."

The uniformed human swore under his breath, and then moved his hand from the weapon. "We don't want this to get any more out of hand. There's nothing here for you to report."

Jacob stepped forward. Kali watched as Trahaearn finally moved away from the door. He was going to join the reporter.

"Officer," he said, "can we settle this without more violence?"

The officer narrowed his eyes. Kali felt the war of emotions within the man's soul. He was glad of the help. The druid seemed to shed calm over the crowd. But he was wearing the uniform, so he was the authority here.

"As I said, we'll need to take statements before anyone leaves. We need to talk to anyone inside that building. The crime scene team will be here soon. You," he pointed to Jacob. "Make sure you get a shot of everyone here. We'll want to match statements with faces."

Panic lanced through Kali as she lost the connection to the

humans she had controlled only minutes before. Next time she would be stronger before she acted. Next time she would groom her disciples so they would not need as much of her energy to control them. Next time there would be more than two deaths.

She observed the action as the uniformed humans asked questions. She was pleased to notice more of her followers slip away before the officers could speak to them. Kali knew that all the statements were a waste of time. No one would remember, if they had even seen, who crushed the two humans. This crime would not be solved.

As small as it was, she would count this as the first of her victories.

Trahaearn leaned against the wall. Things were getting out of hand. It had been so short a time since the change, only three days, but here were the first deaths. At least it was the first deaths he'd witnessed, even if it was just the aftermath. There had been others immediately after the glow started, deaths of Real Folk.

Everything he knew about Kali told him she must be behind it. Her need for death was forcing her to act on the humans and amplify their fear of the unknown.

He stepped down to the grass as soon as it seemed that the police had control. People on the edges of the clearing continued to slip into the trees avoiding official notice as the collective mood calmed. They would be back. Kali had influenced them once, and the second time would be easier. Perhaps they would have some luck and Kali would not know that fact.

He desperately wanted to reach into the earth with his magic and send a calming spell over the crowd. If they had the trust of the humans, it would only be a matter of a spell to show an image of what had happened. But it was too soon to reveal the nature of the Real Folk. Now, more than ever, the announcement had to be controlled.

Trahaearn couldn't stop the feeling that they were standing on a rope hanging above two worlds. On one side was a world of cooperation and trust. On the other a smoking pit of death and pain. The responsibility for the future was his, and he was unprepared.

Moving toward the officer who seemed to be in charge, Trahaearn asked, "Is there anything I can do to help?"

The officer looked at him with suspicion, almost a magical power that seemed to cut through Trahaearn's soul.

Apparently deciding there was nothing to pin this feeling on, the officer said, "Ambulances are on the way for the injured. The coroner is coming for the dead. Did you see anything?"

Thankful he could be truthful, Trahaearn answered, "I came out when I heard the noise of the crowd. The two unfortunate souls were already on the ground."

The officer grunted in acknowledgement. "We'll be investigating this area for a few hours. Please keep your people from interfering. I'll need to talk to anyone inside who might have seen what happened."

Trahaearn knew he couldn't let the police inside. Glen and Angela would not be happy with anyone knowing they were in there. As it stood, he would have to let Lionel do magic to allow the humans to go on their way while the police remained in the clearing.

He wouldn't reveal the other exits. He couldn't endanger the people inside. "I will make sure no one interferes, but I cannot allow you into the building. Some of my brothers are ill, and such disturbance would set back their recovery."

"I can get a warrant," the policeman said.

"As you can see, there are no windows. No one could have seen what was happening outside."

"We'll see what a judge has to say about that," the man said.

Jacob moved between them before Trahaearn could respond. "Will you give me an interview?"

He wanted Jacob to come inside, and it would help when Angela and Glen needed to leave. "Of course, come in."

The cop shook his head in disbelief. "The press is likely to make more problems than we already have. Be careful of what you say."

Trahaearn thanked him and led Jacob into the museum.

When they were behind the closed door, Trahaearn stopped to touch it and send a message to the guardian trees. Their magic may be fading, but he didn't want to delay the ambulance, so he asked them to guide any uniformed humans to the clearing.

"You just glowed." Jacob reached out his hand, pulling back just before making contact. "Sorry, I just wanted to see if it felt different from Dionne's. You glow green."

Ignoring the unspoken request to touch him, Trahaearn asked, "What will we do now about our announcement?"

"Unless we have a way out that the cops can't see, I guess we hold back until the clearing is empty. I'll make some calls, then we can join the others." He moved to the side, holding his phone up to check on the strength of the signal.

Trahaearn went in search of Lionel and Dionne. They were in the kitchen waiting for the kettle to boil. Gareth was peeling potatoes slowly, clearly having to think about each movement. Trahaearn feared that the healing process was going to be more difficult than he expected. The man swung from almost normal to deeply disturbed several times in a day. He would not be able to count on his druids to help. Lionel and Dionne were his only allies from the Real Folk.

"Where are Angela and Glen?" he asked.

Dionne looked up from the tray she was preparing. "We asked them to stay in the room, just in case. They didn't argue. I think they are worried about the implications of being seen leaving here now that there's a problem outside."

Trahaearn gave them an update. "So, we will delay the announcement. And I'll need some kind of invisibility charm to send our guests home."

Lionel poured the boiling water over the tea and placed the lid on the pot. "I can do that. Dionne still needs to be... unglowing? I guess we need a word for that. Anyway, I can build a glamor on them so they fade into the background. If they are careful not to bring attention, they can get out to the streets and go back to do whatever they need to prepare."

"I'll take that with me," Trahaearn said, reaching for the tray. "Dionne, you need some rest. Jacob will let us know when we should get ready."

She sighed, and then laughed. "Sorry. I guess I don't want to miss anything, but I can't risk messing up because I'm tired." She headed for the stairs leading to the sleeping rooms. Trahaearn left Lionel to his preparations, glad of the opportunity to talk to the humans alone.

Jacob was still on his phone as Trahaearn passed through the hall to the small room where the two politicians waited.

9

The druid was outside. Now Kali had her chance. The power she needed to step back into the world in her physical form came from deaths in the normal course of events. Enough had come while she had waited beyond the veil. Checking to make sure no one was present, she manifested in the corridor of the museum.

The building stank of knowledge, and caring, and weakness.

There were humans here. She could smell the ambition coming from the small room to the left. Two humans. Would they both see her? Did she have the power to control both for long enough to get her way?

It was too big a risk. Kali drew in the scent of ambition and targeted the human who fed on it. Sending a command to the woman, to sleep, Kali moved into the room.

"What are you doing?" the man asked as he reached to shake the woman who was resting on the table. "Angela, what is wrong with you?"

"The druid did that," Kali said capturing the man's attention. Fear replaced ambition. Good. She could use that. When he obeyed her first order, this human would become her weapon.

"What kind of being are you?" the man asked regaining some of his arrogance.

"I am Kali. There is no other like me." She spread her arms as she spoke, showing the radiance of her clothing and power with the gesture. "I am here to save you from the druid. He is not what you believe him to be." This man was different from the others. He couldn't be pushed by envy because he was confident, and he believed himself to be someone to be envied. Pride would help when she had him in her control.

"We are aware that he is one of the Real Folk."

Kali laughed. "What is your name wise one?" If the man thought he understood druids, he was in for a shock.

"Glen Watson. What do you want?"

"I want to help free you from the shackles this druid is preparing for you. I want to show you the evil in the Real Folk. I want to help you to win the war that is coming."

The words didn't have as much affect as she expected. What had the druid done to this human? Or had she chosen the wrong one?

"Why should I believe you?" His words were brave, but Kali saw the doubt, the fear of what Trahaearn and the Real Folk could be.

"Why do you believe the druid? Is it because he looks like you? Like a human? How do you know that is his real face? You should trust me because I come to you in my true form." Her energy was slipping away, but Kali knew that she had to be subtle, no matter that it was slow.

"What do you want from me?" Glen leaned back in his chair as though he was negotiating with an equal.

Kali struggled to hide the rage inside. She wanted to kill this human, to replace the energy that he stole with his words, to show him her power, to use him as a tool to build fear in the other human. But she knew that he was going to be more use than just a bloody demonstration for one human. "You must kill the druid before he enslaves you."

Glen frowned in thought as though considering his counteroffer. His arrogance was as attractive as it was infuriating. With such a man as her tool, she would walk the blood-soaked soil of this world without care.

"Why are you fading?" he asked.

Kali could feel the veil reaching out to pull her back. "I will return to you soon. Remember my words. He will enslave you with the power he wields. You have no armor against him. No weapon that will defeat him if you allow the druid to continue." She felt the veil close around her as she spoke the last words.

Trahaearn pushed open the door to the meeting room, tray in hand. His senses were alerted to danger by the coppery smell of blood, then a glimpse of Kali as she faded into nothing. He placed the tray on the table next to Angela. As he reached to check her pulse, she gave a quiet snore. Turning to check Glen, Trahaearn noticed the man's skin was sallow and his eyes unfocused. Kali had taken him away from the world.

Now he had no choice but to use magic, he only hoped that Jacob could deal with the resulting glow as part of their announcement. Trahaearn reached out to touch Glen's temple, ready to sense for life inside. As soon as Trahaearn's fingers made contact, Glen shuddered and the light returned to his eyes.

"Who was that?" he asked.

Trahaearn motioned for Glen to sit and then poured some tea, leaving Angela to her dreams for the meantime. "Tell me what you saw. What you remembered."

Glen picked up the mug of tea in shaking hands. He sipped before answering. "A blue woman, her tongue was sticking out. That was odd because I heard everything she said clearly. She was dressed ornately, in a sari, or something like that."

There was no doubt it had been Kali.

"I only know her as Kali. There are creatures, beings, possibly gods, who live just outside our world. They can come into this world and they are... the best word is responsible for certain aspects of our lives. Kali is our current goddess of fertility and death. She seems very focused on death at the moment."

Glen glanced at Angela. "And what other magic does she have? This is one of your Magical Beings?"

"She is not Real Folk, and she is not someone we can control." Trahaearn could hear Jacob's voice drawing near. "Perhaps we can keep this between us for now. I think her existence can only complicate matters."

The appeal to Glen's need to be important worked.

"Well we cannot keep it secret for long. If she came to me, she'll be coming to others. But I believe you are right; it is a complication we do not need at this time."

Trahaearn woke Angela just as Jacob entered the room. Dionne ran in behind Jacob. "Things are getting out of control. Someone set a fire in the forest. I saw it online. Can we find out if anyone is hurt?"

Their time was up.

"Yes, but we need to get this press conference done. We cannot stop the coming storm until we are known to the humans."

"Wait, let me see what I can find out," Jacob said. "I doubt we'll know if any Real Folk were killed, but I can get more details than were posted online." He didn't wait for an answer, just took out his phone and made a call.

"I seem to have missed something," Angela said. "I don't know why I fell asleep, but Glen and I will need to leave soon. Is the trouble outside resolved?"

Too many things were happening, and Trahaearn could feel the weight of the secrets he was starting to accumulate. He reported on the events outside the museum while Jacob talked to his contact. "Lionel will make sure you are able to leave unnoticed soon."

Dionne was vibrating with worry. Trahaearn reached to touch her and offer some calm, he was worried about the friends he'd made, and about the retaliation that might come if someone had died in the fire.

"Okay, yes. Someone started a fire in the park, but it got put out before it burned much. I think your friends are fine, but you should still check."

"We do need to leave," Glen said. "What is Lionel doing to allow that? I have no wish to be recorded leaving here until we have given a coordinated message."

The man really did have the ambition it took to be a leader. Half the time Trahaearn found himself admiring Glen and the other half of the time he was repelled.

"Dionne, check to see if Lionel is ready," he said. Then, turning to Angela and Glen, Trahaearn continued, "He has a charm for you to place in your pocket. When you leave, the spell fades you into the background. Go carefully and no one will notice you."

Glen was the first to speak. "How do we know that this is not an attempt to control us?"

Trahaearn knew that it would take time for their trust to become solid. It would be the same for him in reversed circumstances. The distrust only delayed them, but each time he explained, it strengthened the growing relationship.

"If that is what we wished, you would be under our power already. The magic is in the charm. Drop it in a drain or something when it is safe for you to be seen." He saw something glimmer in Angela's eyes at the information. "The magic will expire in a few hours regardless of what you do with the charms."

Angela chuckled. "Well, I suppose a little spying would be wrong. Just know that there are those among us who would use that kind of spell for their own ends."

Dionne returned with a small bag. "He's done it. Here are the charms." She emptied the bag onto the table. Two walnuts spun and then came to rest. "They will work on the first person to touch them, and only on that person."

The two politicians took the charms. To Trahaearn's eyes, they simply shimmered.

"Holy shit," Jacob gasped out. "They just disappeared."

"No. They blend in," Dionne said pointing toward the wall. "It doesn't work on Real Folk as well as it does on humans. We can see them, but you can't."

Jacob stepped forward, hand reaching out.

Angela's voice brought him to a stop. "Don't get any closer. You are about to touch the wrong part of me."

"Sorry," he said taking a step back. "Look, we can do the conference tomorrow at the same time as it was supposed to be today. It might be better now anyway. It's good no one got hurt, but a little drama will go a long way to get the public's attention."

Trahaearn ignored the glee in Jacob's voice. "If you have anything more to contribute, let's get to it. The others can't just open the door and leave if they are invisible. You'll be their cover."

Jacob didn't seem to notice the annoyance in Trahaearn's tone. "Nope, I have what I need. I'll check with you tomorrow about the key points we'll need to include in the press conference. I'll prep Glen and Angela. We'll text Dionne with the details."

Trahaearn made sure the police outside saw him say goodbye to Jacob keeping their attention away from the two people who slipped through the door and wove through the crowd that was still moving around the clearing.

10

Kali slipped through the veil and found the druid alone.

She was still weak and that frightened her. With all the evil in this world, all the sickness, and all the hatred, she should be fed with a constant stream of power. It seemed that the humans everywhere were pausing to find out what happened in this small area of the world. When she was victorious, she would have to find out why this was so powerful a city.

"I am winning, druid," she announced as she flowed into the world. "Cede me your power now, and I will spare some of your friends."

The druid turned to face her. It galled that he showed no fear. His face filled with contempt, and pity. The pity was worse.

"Kali, you will not be victorious. What happens when you kill everyone? Have you thought about that? When there is no one to suffer, you will have no power."

She laughed feeling glorious in her ability to fool these naive beings. "I will have sufficient power for centuries if I choose to rid this world of the vermin. But death is not the only thing that gives me power. I will husband my resources, do not concern yourself with my future."

The druid was skilled at keeping his thoughts from his face, but Kali was learning to read the inner person. Like she had with her disciples who formed the mob outside.

The druid was afraid. Afraid that she would find allies in the humans and the magical beings.

Yes, that was a good plan. She would bring all kinds of followers to her cause.

"The deaths outside your door brought attention you did not anticipate," she said, gliding closer.

He took a seat at the table. "Was two deaths enough?"

Kali knew he was not as relaxed as he intended her to believe. "For now. As proof I can control these humans, yes the first two deaths were enough." Her lie flowed easily. In truth, they had cost her more power than they gave. The druid did not need to know that.

"We will find a way to diminish your power. We will live with the humans as a family." Trahaearn pushed his chair away from the table, tipped it back, and raised his legs to rest his heels on the tabletop. "This war you are determined to start will not give you the power you need, Kali. It is in all of our interests that you find a balance between life and death. Your power comes from the joy of sex and birth as much as from pain and death. The Morrigan filled your role for centuries by doing just that."

The foul druid was insolent.

Kali drew on her small reserve of power and used it to close the man's throat. The surprise on his face was almost as energizing as death power. She needed him to believe that she could end his life, before she slipped back through the veil. Her real lack of energy must remain hidden from him.

"I am not your Morrigan. If she was so powerful, I would not be here. I would still be...." The thought of her past broke her hold on Trahaearn's throat. He gasped in air, his body curling around itself to protect it from further harm.

What had she been before?

Was there a before?

Kali couldn't recall. It seemed to her that she had sprung to life as the old goddess passed. But now a worm of doubt twisted inside. Had there been a before? Had she failed at her task and been exiled to this realm?

"Would still be where?" the druid wheezed out. "Or what, Kali? What were you before?"

The words resonated with her own question. This was not the place to show how little she knew. "Do not question me, druid. I will spare your life for now. If you persist in this foolish plan for peace, you will feel the pain of loss. I will take those close to you first, then every being on this world before I take you. Consider how that will damage you."

Not waiting for his response, she faded out of the world.

TRAHAEARN RUBBED HIS THROAT. THERE WAS NO PAIN, BUT HE felt as though there should be. Kali was gaining in skill if not in power. Power would not be too far behind. Things were not going his way, and that had to change.

The day was still young. He could use Dionne and Lionel to check on the forest folk, if they hadn't already thought to do that. Then he would get Dionne to show him how to read the news on her phone. Knowledge was power, and when the police were gone, they needed as much knowledge as possible to make their announcement a success.

He searched the building for Dionne and Lionel and found them in the basement. He waited a few steps from the bottom as the two cleared the circle. When the magic was dissipated, he continued to the bare earth.

Lionel was glowing, but Dionne had remembered her role and stayed away from casting spells. He knew that must irk her. Having just come into her power, she would seek every opportunity to use it. She would get enough practice over the next few days, as every human demanded a sample of magic. Eventually, she would tire of casting spells.

She noticed Trahaearn as his feet touched the earth. "Everyone is okay. The fire didn't get near Beacon's camp."

"Good. Did they have any other news?" Trahaearn beckoned them up the stairs. They both looked more tired than he expected.

"Nothing. It's only been an hour since the fire was put out," Lionel answered.

His words brought Trahaearn to a stop. "It's been only a few minutes."

"No, it's been about an hour. We had to work hard to find someone who would come to our call. Everyone is afraid that the humans will find a way to penetrate a circle and then kill the Real Folk at the other side."

Kali had stolen time from him.

Trahaearn understood why Lionel looked like he'd been drained of magic. Casting for an hour under this amount of stress would drain anyone, let alone someone two days free of the same prison that the druid souls had endured. It was a miracle that Lionel could function at all.

"That is a concern. I was visited by Kali. We need to find out what her human legend is and try to mitigate her actions." Trahaearn knew that the human legend may not help them, but it would be knowledge. If it meant sending someone to a human library, then he needed to spare one of these two.

Gareth waited at the head of the stairs. Trahaearn had heard nothing of the man's approach. A healthy druid would make no noise if he wanted to be silent. It was good that Gareth was testing his boundaries, but Trahaearn realized he needed to be more alert to what was happening around him. "Gareth, how are the others?"

"They are restless, as if they are fighting someone." The druid looked to Trahaearn like a child asking for help.

"Set protective wards." If Kali was trying to possess his druids, she might succeed. Their minds were healing from their imprisonment, so their own barriers would be weak. There were too many things to be responsible for when he needed desperately to stop the world from falling into chaos. It might have only been a day and a half, but events were rushing forward. He considered Kali's ability to enter this world through normal wards. "Make them the strongest we have, and, Gareth, give them something to deepen their sleep. Perhaps that will keep Kali away from them."

Gareth nodded and moved toward the kitchen.

Suddenly worried that Kali had taken the man, Trahaearn asked, "Have you been visited by any angry blue women lately?"

Gareth turned, a wicked grin on his face. "She tried to enlist me in her plans. I suggested we test our alliance with a night of passion. It did not sit well with her. Perhaps she knows how long it has been since I had a woman. A single night might not be enough."

Trahaearn heard Dionne giggle behind him. He turned to see Lionel blushing. Looking back at Gareth, Trahaearn said, "If she comes to you again, keep making the offer. Perhaps a taste of druid lovemaking will soften her mood."

Knowing that his only lucid druid was strong enough to be proof against treachery lifted a little of the weight on Trahaearn's shoulders. "Let's prepare for this conference as much as we can. I intend to get this over with, so we know what allies we have and where we are weak. We cannot let more time slip by."

The front door opened, and Trahaearn noticed that both Lionel and Dionne had reached for charms to use on the intruder. He was about to chide them when he realized his own hand was curled ready to draw magic for a spell.

This was not the way to make peace. No one who could open that door so easily was an enemy.

"There's a problem," Jacob said as he slipped inside.

Trahaearn beckoned him to the small room he had come to

think of as the war room. "What now? We need to take control, not keep running to and fro pushed by the actions of others."

Jacob lifted his backpack from his shoulders and placed it on the table, rolling his neck as though the bag carried the weight of the world instead of his computer and camera.

"There's this preacher in the Valley. He's a bit of a nut, but now he's started talking about evil and seeing demons. He's claiming that humans will become slaves to the demons. We'll know them because they glow with an unholy light."

"That's crazy," Dionne said, exasperation showing in her tight face and the wave of her hands. "No one is going to listen to that guy. You are talking about the Reverend Jeremiah Nielson, right? The guy who predicted The Rapture?"

Trahaearn watched as Jacob shook his head. He wasn't denying Dionne's identification. It was frustration and a world-weariness beyond the man's years. "People are getting scared. They'll believe anyone who promises to keep them safe no matter the cost. And we are going to have to fight that image when we reveal you to the world."

"Who is this man?" Trahaearn wasn't ready to take on a new threat, but he knew that's not how it worked. If he wasn't informed, he couldn't manage the fallout. There would be fallout because he was certain Kali was involved. She was behind every barrier they faced. "How can we deflect his influence?"

Jacob held up his phone. "I have some dirt on him. I've got a post ready to go that shines a light on his little vices. If we can make him look less than pure, people won't be so eager to follow him."

Dionne sucked in a breath. "Isn't that feeding the trolls?"

Lionel voiced the concern in Trahaearn's mind. "Trolls? Have people seen them?"

She laughed. "Sorry, human term. Trolls are people who just like to jump in with a lot of hateful stuff whenever they have the opportunity. Feeding the trolls means giving them attention. If you ignore them, they eventually go away. If you feed them, they go into a frenzy."

"Real Folk trolls are not like that," Trahaearn said. He chose to follow Dionne's approach to dealing with this latest problem. "I think we ignore him and come out with our announcement as soon as we possibly can."

Jacob looked at his phone and touched the screen. "Sorry, I have to post it. My followers will expect me to use the information. Most of it came from them."

Trahaearn bit back the anger at Jacob's casual action. Expressing his anger now could do more damage to their relationship than the satisfaction it would bring. It was an effect of this hiding in the shadows. Before the prophecy there were two parallel paths. Neither the humans nor the Real Folk hid in shadows, they simply lived their lives. Now, and until the truth was published, the Real Folk cowered in the forest, figuratively and literally.

It did worry him that Jacob wasn't held obedient by the oath. If humans were not bound by their word, this new world would be a dangerous place for Real Folk for a very long time.

"Then we need to answer with the truth now. Can you arrange for our friends to join us so that we can finalize the speeches?"

Jacob touched his phone again and spoke as he moved it to his ear. "I'm not sure how many times they will come here at your request. Is it possible for you to leave? You aren't glowing — well, except for Lionel." The call was answered before Trahaearn could respond.

Was he confident that they could leave the museum? Was it reasonable to keep asking two people with political influence to come to him?

Jacob looked at Trahaearn. "I'm on hold. What do you think about meeting at city hall?"

"We have to leave at some point," Trahaearn said. "It has only been two days, but it is very much starting to feel like that is two days too late. I'll find more appropriate clothing. The robe is likely to draw attention before we want it."

KALI TRIED TO IGNORE THE TUG AT HER BEING. SOMETHING was calling her. Somehow, she had given someone the power to summon her.

Fighting it was taking energy she couldn't spare, so Kali let the summons drag her to its source. She would deal with the person who acted in such a disrespectful way when she knew how they had managed to gain this ability. And their death would make up for the drain on her power.

She felt a constant hunger for the life force that should be flowing freely.

The world that faded into view was the office of that preacher. Kali slipped into the image of his saint and greeted him. "You have need of me?" Her voice was meek, easily hiding the fury that rose in her at the realization that she had given him the power to call her.

And what if it were everyone who had acted on her behalf? They were her believers and that gave them power. She would have to take care in how she used the humans in the future. Kali had no plans to be at the beck and call of a horde of followers.

"I worry that I am not doing as you need," Jeremiah said.

His words were also meek, but they were delivered with a strength that worried her. Another thing she would have to investigate when she had the strength. Was her influence on those she had already captured, strong enough?

"There is one who stands in opposition to the light I bring." Kali would use this tool now that he had the power to summon her.

"You wish me to help you with this? Simply tell me the name of this unbeliever and I will remove the barrier." There was a gleam in Jeremiah's eye as he made the offer. If he was hungry for the kill, she would be more lenient with him when she took power. A man willing to sacrifice for her would be worth a little mercy.

"It is a man. He is preparing to fill the world with his lies." She kept her image humble, eyes downcast, voice gentle. The real emotions she felt, the hunger for death, the joy at the thought of the druid being slaughtered, the ecstasy at the very thought of the terror that could be released with his pain and humiliation, would turn Jeremiah away from her.

"I can discredit him before he utters one lie. I can turn his followers to me. Tell me who this man is, and I will gladly bring him down."

His reaction confirmed her hopes. Jeremiah was gleeful at the thought of destroying an adversary. She struggled to keep her victorious smile from bleeding into the image of the saint. "I have more need for you than simply destroying this man. I would have you reason with him. I have other followers who would end this man if needed. We do not wish to be rash," she counseled as a new plan formed in her mind. "I will return to tell you where to be so that you can speak with his audience."

Jeremiah knelt and looked up at her. Kali wondered at the greed in his expression, was that what piety really was?

"I am yours to command," Jeremiah said.

Kali felt herself losing control of the image. It was not yet time to reveal her true self to this man. He was not yet hers completely. "Prepare yourself. I will transport you to the man when the time is right," she said as she faded away.

Now she had to store energy to move his mass to wherever the druid was going to make his brave and stupid appeal for harmony.

Kali allowed the cackle of joy to escape as soon as she was fully past the veil.

❧ 11 ❧

Trahaearn looked around the room.

Honey colored wood covered the walls three quarters of the way to the ceiling. Cream paint filling the remainder of the wall. The ceiling was coffered with the same wood. Someone with a love for nature had decorated this room. In fact, the whole interior of the building felt like it had been designed by sprites and sidhe. The outside consisted of concrete and small windows — it gave off an aura of cold importance and represented all that was human.

This room was Angela's office at City Hall. They were here to refine their plans before going in front of the cameras and shocking the world with the revelation of a whole magical life that was previously unknown.

It was difficult to sit and listen to them solve problems that only humans would cause. Dionne did her best to add clarity, but her youth gave her a skewed perspective.

Finally at the end of his patience, Trahaearn asked, "What exactly is the problem? I understand that it is important for everyone to have a voice, but why can we not just hold this press conference, each speak our part and then deal with what comes of it?" He suspected that he knew the answer but hoped he could break the circle of arguments that kept them from moving forward.

Glen was the first to speak. "It is not simply the revelation of a whole world that parallels ours, but a political statement. There are three messages we need to get out: that you exist is the first, that you are not the enemy is the second. And it would be better coming from the mayor, or the Premier, or even the Prime Minister. But they are in conference right now trying to work out the bigger ramifications. The third message is how you can help us."

Trahaearn knew what the titles meant. The humans liked many layers of government. The mayor led city, the Premier ran the province, and the Prime Minister the country. He hoped they would not cause new problems while he was dealing with the announcement.

"And we are not willing to lose the political edge this gives us," Angela added. "I am sorry to be so blunt, but it is the truth and if we face it then we can move faster."

Jacob busied himself with making some final changes to the speaking points. He seemed willing to take the back seat on the publicity, but Trahaearn knew full well that Jacob's career would be made by this announcement. He could become the official communication person for all of the Real Folk.

Damn, he needed to stop thinking of them by that name. The *Magical Beings* was the expression that they'd agreed to and he needed to be an example to the other Real...Magical beings.

Glen sat back in his chair, raised his left leg to rest the ankle on his right knee, the image of relaxation. "Yes, but if we are going to speak plainly, let's acknowledge the other two concerns we have. We do not wish to be smeared with the fallout if this goes wrong, and some of us have religious considerations as well as political. Leaders of every religion will need to be reassured."

Trahaearn gritted his teeth. It was becoming too complicated for them to make progress. "How do you intend to be part of this and take credit as well as avoid blame?" He'd leave the religious leaders out of it for the moment.

Angela laughed, a bitter sound. "That is what we do as politicians, druid. I am very surprised you have no experience with that. If your magical beings are not capable of subtlety, then they will not last long in the human world."

Before Trahaearn could answer that, Glen said, "Nothing about us is simple. Any problem that can be solved simply will be battered with self-interest until it is possible to have the same outcome be both a win and a loss. You should feel grateful, Trahaearn, that you are simply waiting for something violent to happen and not already dealing with the aftermath. Your prophecy must have something to do with it. I am surprised that no one has bombed the hell out of anything that glows, that no one has been burned at the stake, that... well you get the idea."

Trahaearn couldn't argue against history. And he knew full well that nothing was one-dimensional. In the Real... the magical beings' normal world, they stayed out of each other's business as much as possible. He just wished that Glen's eyes hadn't gleamed when he listed the retribution that they were trying to avoid, as if he regretted that it would not happen. "The sidhe have enough political savvy for all of us, but we are not strangers to this. My experience has been that you cannot prepare for everything. I will be the one who speaks, that should take care of the blame. You can measure the response and do as you feel fit."

Taking the speaking notes from Jacob, Trahaearn urged everyone to practice their parts during this hour before they told the world the truth.

THERE WAS A CROWD IN THE FOYER OF THE BUILDING. THREE crowds in fact. The one facing them was tightly packed, camera flashes periodically blinding Trahaearn. A murmur of eagerness and hunger flowed toward him. The second stood behind the reporters and flowed onto the street. They held placards and chanted different objections, from religious issues to pleas to save the planet, to something about saving jobs. Their actions seemed to be aimed as much at the reporters as at Trahaearn.

The third group stood beside and slightly behind him, just out of camera range. Other politicians. He knew they were there to steal the glory if everything went right. If things went wrong, they would disappear as if they had never been there.

Jacob had briefed Trahaearn on maintaining the spotlight so he could control the message. As much as he'd wanted to get this over with before, Trahaearn found himself fighting not to run.

Jacob leaned across Dionne. "You need to get started or the crowd will take over. Tap the microphone and they'll shut up."

Resisting the urge to cast a spell of calm, Trahaearn did as directed and the crowd of reporters quieted. The protestors didn't stop chanting until two uniformed officers moved in closer.

Into the silence, Trahaearn started his speech. "We thank you for your patience. I have a short statement to make, and my colleague will be performing a demonstration. After that we'll address any questions you may have." He paused and glanced across the faces in front of him. They were ready to hear him.

Trahaearn ignored the people around him. They would do as they needed. He had argued for the information to be shared boldly and now he had to say the words. A chill of fear was a surprise to him, this wasn't the first time he'd addressed a group, but it was the first time he'd been in the presence of so many humans.

"Two days ago, an event changed the entire world. You have all noticed the evidence as a glow. I am here to explain what is causing the glow." He paused again for a deep breath. "Until two days ago a world existed that paralleled yours. A world of magical creatures. Now the two worlds have united."

One of the reporters called out, "A magical world, come on."

Trahaearn smiled, Jacob had predicted that response. "We know that is hard to believe, but we can prove it. My colleague, Dionne Walker, will cast a harmless spell which will prove the magic, and you will see the result."

He stepped to the side so that Dionne could take the center spot. She smiled at the audience. "Let me introduce myself, because people will recognize me, and I don't want them too worried. I lived as a human until a while ago. I found out I was magical and it freaked me out to start with. So first, I'd like to say hi to my foster parents and Ms. Metcalfe. I'm really sorry I couldn't tell you what happened to me, but I'm doing great."

She waved at the cameras before continuing. "Okay, so you see I don't glow, right?" When a murmur of acknowledgement reached her, Dionne continued, "I had to be convinced that magic existed and it's hard, right? I mean we're so used to Vegas magicians doing great tricks."

Trahaearn wondered where Dionne had learned to work a crowd so well. Her dramatic pauses and attitude of 'we're all in this together' were making a difference.

Holding out her left arm, she asked, "Just checking again, no glow, right? Okay, I'm going to do some magic. I'm happy to demonstrate more after we're done here, but this should do the trick."

Dionne opened her hand and turned her extended arm so the palm was facing upward. She ran her right index finger from wrist to elbow. As her finger passed, rose petals formed and fell, the rich scent filling the foyer and then evaporating. There was movement at the very back of the crowd as protestors leaned forward to catch the act.

Dionne drew her finger back and a rainbow of sparks scattered.

Trahaearn heard a gasp as someone noticed the glow intensify.

She wasn't finished. When the sparks flickered out, Dionne held her palm out higher and smoke rose from her skin. The smoke swirled, creating patterns that blended together finally forming an image of a fairy.

"This is Bud, the Queen of the rose fairies," she said, then motioned and the image fluttered its wings and flew out of the chamber. "And you can see that I'm giving off enough light to read by."

There was silence.

They had prepared for every eventuality except this nothing.

Trahaearn moved to stand beside Dionne. He prepared a defensive spell in his mind just in case this went horribly wrong. "Any questions?"

Before any of the reporters could ask, a voice came from the back of the room. "This is the devil's work." The speaker was a large man, his face flushed with anger or fear, or both.

"Shit," Jacob uttered. "Jeremiah Nielson, just what we didn't need."

"I assure you we are not evil," Trahaearn said. This was not the place to debate religious philosophy. "We are hoping to meet with your religious leaders soon."

"I have been visited by a saint. She told me to fight this madness. That these are not God's children." Jeremiah's voice rose. He was not going to be distracted.

Hoping to maintain control of the message they needed the world to understand, Trahaearn turned to the reporters. "I'm sure you have questions."

One hand went up. "How do we know you won't cast spells on us to control us?"

At least they had prepared for this one. "I can assure you that we have no intention of controlling you. Our worlds have been close for as long as we can remember. We have been aware of humans the entire time. We have never attacked you before. We have no interest in taking power away. We only wish to coexist in harmony."

"The devil makes promises too," Jeremiah shouted.

The reporters looked to Trahaearn for a response. "We have done nothing to you in the last two days. We have withdrawn to protect ourselves. If our goal was to take over your world, why would we come in front of you to explain?"

There were some nods from the crowd. Others looked to Jeremiah for more meat to include in the story. Trahaearn could sense the three crowds were balanced between emotion and evidence right now. It would take only a gentle push to turn it into a riot, or keep it civilized. Jacob had carefully timed the announcement just for this moment.

"I believe you all have deadlines to meet," Trahaearn said to the reporters. "If any of you wish a private interview, please speak to our representative." He pointed to Jacob and then took Dionne's arm and turned away.

"You will not bring demons to this land," Jeremiah ranted. "Whatever you have unleashed will be defeated by the army of God."

KALI WATCHED THE CIRCUS PLAYING OUT OVER THE DRUID'S announcement of peace and harmony. She remained behind the veil and was glad of it when she saw Jeremiah perform like a madman. She almost spat out her anger. The fool was going to ruin everything with his ranting. Sure, he'd bring some people to the cause, but he would only bring the mad to the battle. That was short-lived power and the most easily overcome.

She needed someone who could create a following, someone who would bring worshipers. She watched as Jeremiah was drawn to the side by two uniformed men and wondered if she could nudge them into killing the man. Deciding that he might have his uses later, even if only to bring fodder to the death orgy she'd create, Kali turned her focus elsewhere.

In the corner of the room, keeping out of the commotion that sprang up when the druid left, was a familiar mind. One of the men she'd taken to cause the riot outside the druid's hovel. This one had a complex mind. He would do well, but this was not the place to influence him. She could not show herself here and expect people to listen. Her presence would cause panic, and, as pleasant that was to imagine, it was another short-lived power source. Kali was tired of being at the mercy of her hunger.

The uniformed men and women managed to create some order and then started moving people outside, calming them and threatening incarceration at the same time. If only they didn't shine with good will, she could turn them to her purposes.

Her target waited until there was a gap in the flow of people before slipping out and avoiding the notice of the authorities. Good. Slyness would be an asset.

Kali drifted after him keeping her energy use low as he purposely walked to a house ten minutes away. The man entered the house with Kali following. As soon as they were alone, she allowed her voice to cross the veil.

"You are a wise man," she whispered. "You deserve power. I can give it to you." She felt no need to be subtle. In her short experience, she'd learned that men didn't respond to it anyway.

He spun around looking for the source of the voice. The man rubbed his temples as he searched the hidden places of the room, behind the furniture, on the other side of the door across from him, even under the sofa.

When she thought he was clear that there was no one hiding, she spoke again. "You are not going mad. I am real. What is your name?"

He sat on the sofa and placed his head in his hands, his spirit dull with some defeat she couldn't understand.

"Randall Bluth. But you know that. You are just the same voices in my head. I guess my medication isn't working."

Kali shimmered the veil in front of Randall, easing her image through. "I am not a voice in your head. I am Kali, the goddess of this world."

Randall's head snapped up toward her image. "Hallucinations are new. Why would I imagine a Hindu goddess?" He reached out to touch her robes.

Kali did not like to be touched. It leached some of her power. But this Randall needed to be sure that she was real. Allowing him to feel her sari could be worth the small drain on her energy.

His fingertips brushed against the silk and he jerked them back as though her clothes were fire.

His fear more than made up for the tiny loss of energy.

"You believe I am real? That the announcement today was not a fabrication?"

Randall's gaze was unblinking. Kali felt a war of emotions running through his energy.

Fear. He knew her legend and was right to be fearful.

Awe. Yes, he was willing to join her and bring others.

Greed, and pride, and cruelty rose to the top of his spirit. And something else. She didn't know what, but it seemed he'd already acted against the magical ones. Yes. She had chosen the right man.

"Will you lead my followers? Will you stop this druid who only seeks to enslave you?"

A gleam of zealous loyalty overshadowed his fear and awe. "Me? Yes, if you want me, I will lead your followers. I will make the world believe in you. I will help you to defeat that man, or whatever he claims to be, and his entire world."

Kali smiled. She hadn't realized that worship could feed her. It was not as sustaining as death, but it was constant when it came. She had difficulty seeing Randall Bluth as a man through the blaze of adoration. It had been easy, but she wasn't worried. It should be easy with the right people.

"I must return to where I am needed," she said. "Prepare and bring others to our cause. I will come back to you when the time is right."

Randall knelt and bowed his head in prayer.

As she faded out Kali heard the words. "Whatever will bring you power, Great Kali. Whatever I can do to vanquish your enemies, I will do gladly."

His fervor was both gratifying and worrying. Had it been too easy? Was there something in her presence that intensified his adoration? Kali watched for long minutes to see if Randall would lose his fire, but nothing changed. And, more importantly, nothing felt like it was giving him power over her.

"Is that it?" Trahaearn asked as they entered Angela's office. "I thought there would be more questions, arguments, anything but that." He waved his hand toward the lobby.

Jacob laughed. "Not on your life. That guy just distracted the press for a minute. I'm happy he showed up. I was worried that they would be so shocked that there would be no questions, and that means no press. Give it a few minutes and the interview requests will come flooding in."

"I don't have time to do multiple interviews. Can we just do one that covers every question?" He needed to start settling the details. How people would live together without friction. How the Real... the magical folk would integrate — or not.

Angela pointed to an empty seat. "Just rest. Dionne must be tired, and we still have to find a way to get you home without too much fuss. I've asked for a police escort."

Trahaearn sat next to Dionne and checked her state. She was excited and nervous, not tired. He saw the glow was fading; good it would help them to slip out.

"And the interviews? How many will we need to do, and how long before we start bringing humans and magical folk together?"

Jacob placed his phone on the table and pointed to it. "See, there are already ten texts from bookers. You'll need to do all of the legitimate outlets. Eventually you'll need to do the US ones too, but for now let's get on the more levelheaded ones."

Glen remained by the door, as if ready to leave if the situation changed. "There's only so much we can do to bring people together," he said. "You need to be legally classified as people, in the current environment of inclusion that shouldn't be a problem. Then, as your natural talents are deemed useful, you will find a place in our economy and society."

Trahaearn kept his expression neutral. Why did the man think it was simply a matter of the Real Folk fitting in with human society? Could he not imagine a new combined society? "I must report to the others. How quickly can this escort be ready to take us back to the museum?"

"But what about the interviews?" Jacob asked. "You can't put them off if you want to control the message."

Trahaearn looked to Dionne for confirmation. He knew what would be right in California — to leave. There, it would be a feeding frenzy of crackpots. The noise from the fringe would drown out the rational questions.

She shrugged in response to his glance. "I think he's probably right, but wouldn't it make sense to wait until you have more requests. You can schedule them to our agenda rather than just who's asking."

Jacob looked up from his phone. "There are twenty now, but only a few of the legitimate ones. I'll come to the museum in an hour, hour and a half, with a plan. We can do them one after the other so it's mostly over in one day."

It was more important to get back to the museum right now, Trahaearn thought. If this was how the humans reacted when there were police watching, who knew what was going on at home. Lionel wasn't strong enough, or experienced enough to deal with a mob.

"Then I think we need to go," he said. Turning to Angela, he added, "Would you and Glen join us for the interviews?"

"I'll be there," she answered. "I won't miss an opportunity to show that I'm in the know. I don't speak for Glen."

Trahaearn sensed that Angela had picked up the change in Glen's interest. He turned to look at the man who was checking his watch. "Glen, will you be with us?"

"I will need to check my schedule. Let me know the timing, and I will do my best."

So, he had other things that were suddenly more important than the Real Folk. They would have to be careful with information until they knew his real allegiance.

A quiet knock on the door pulled their attention. The door opened before they could react and a riot-gear clad policeman stepped into the room. Glen slipped out and Trahaearn saw two other similarly dressed men in the hall before the door closed.

The officer nodded to Angela. "The area has been cleared. We should leave now before anyone gets any crazy ideas."

Trahaearn and Dionne followed their escort through the hall to a back door. Angela stayed with them through the door and toward the cruisers sitting in a small parking lot.

As they approached the cruisers, there was a shout.

The officers raised their shields and moved to protect their charges against a man who rushed them, a large curved knife raised over his head.

"Kali, Kali, Kali," the man repeated the name as he ran into the riot shields. His drive to slay his target so intense he didn't seem to recognize the fact that he was stopped by the barrier of heavily clad and armed police.

Two of the officers remained as a wall of protection while the other knocked the knife from the assailant with his riot club. The attacker was on the ground and handcuffed in what felt like seconds.

Trahaearn took Angela and Dionne's arms and drew them back to the door, the two officers maintaining their post even though there were no other attackers present.

"Kali is one of your people?" Angela asked in a faint voice. She leaned against the wall, breathless, eyes wide. "What have you brought to our lives?"

Dionne took the woman's hand. Trahaearn saw the telltale glow as she used her healing power to calm Angela.

"She's not exactly one of us," Dionne said. "There are other beings. But Kali is new and we don't know anything about her."

Trahaearn drew the group behind the waiting police to the safety of the office. When they were settled in relative privacy, he explained the presence of beings such as Kali.

"There are different planes of existence. Humans and Real... Magical Folk live here on this plane together. We, those of us with magical power, are able to travel across the surface of the veil between worlds as we communicate in the circles. Others live in the world beyond the veil, and some of them can pass through to our world."

"And Kali is one of these?" Angela asked. Her composure was back, but she still held an aura of fear.

"Yes, but she is recent. She is the... avatar, I suppose is the best label, of fertility and death on this plane. The last one, The Morrigan, was equally focused on the life generating energies as she was in leading the dead to their next life." He paused, not sure how much needed to be shared.

If he had hours, or days, he could explain more of the realities that humans seemed to be oblivious to. But he needed to get back to the museum and find a way to move forward faster than they were. He knew in a way that felt like prophecy that the balance they had achieved was delicate and the next move could either drop the world into violence and hatred, or into a more healthy harmony. If Kali had managed to influence someone to kill, then time was more precious than he'd thought. The next move had to be from the side of harmony, and the next after that, if they were to prevail.

Deciding to speak only to the matter at hand, he continued, "Kali seems thirsty for death. She will not turn to the other side of her being."

Dionne piped in from her position near the door. "She wants the opposite of our goal. She wants to turn this world into a bloodbath. You know how easy that could be, Angela. Do you know anything about how to stop her?"

Angela shook her head slowly as if searching for an answer. "Our legend is not about how to deal with her. It only tells us that she goes on a campaign of terror. That she is unstoppable until her true love intervenes."

"True love?" Dionne asked Angela. "Could we find him and introduce them?" Then, turning to Trahaearn, she continued, "Is there a spell we can cast? Is it possible he exists? Can we send her to the same place that The Morrigan went?"

He wished the answer were yes to even one of the questions. "We do not know who will replace Kali. These beings are made up of the myths and gods of humans. What if the next one is worse?"

Dionne pulled herself away from the wall. "We can't just wait her out."

Trahaearn held up his hand to stop her as she went to open the door. Then, when she nodded, he turned to the human. "Angela, if we can find Kali's true love, what will happen?"

"If she is tied to the legend, she will remember the good things of life and will not try to turn the world into an ocean of blood." She rose from the chair. "I do not know how you will find him, he is The Lord Shiva, a god."

It figured. Trying to summon a god would take more than the few days they had if it were even possible. Was Kali sent because the prophecy heralded the end of life here? Trahaearn would not accept that. If she had a gentle side, he would find a way to expose it. "Is there nothing in the legend to tell us how to find him?"

Angela picked up her purse and marched to the door. "No, but I will talk to people who may know, and we will find a way. Try to stay alive while you save the world, Trahaearn." She pulled open the door and left without another word.

A uniformed guard approached as Angela turned the corner of the corridor. "It's safe now. We'll drive you home."

"WE NEED TO CALL THE OTHERS TO A CIRCLE," TRAHAEARN said as soon as the museum doors were closed and they were safe in what he was starting to think of as the real world. This world of humans was too full of traps and unfamiliar threats. The world of the amulet was horrific, but at least it was a horror he'd understood. Here, in his museum, he at least felt the illusion of safety.

Lionel appeared at the top of the stairs. The sight of the young wizard made Trahaearn feel guilty at the way he'd minimized the horror of the amulet. Lionel had spent a week there and had gone back to help save the druids trapped for centuries. Unlike the world of the amulet, the humans would eventually come to realize that working together was more profitable, or sensible, or simply safer than fighting. They may have a different understanding of life than the Real Folk do, but their motives, no matter how obscured by fear, had to be similar.

Trahaearn left Dionne to bring Lionel up to date and then instructed them to set the circle. His thoughts reminded him of his duty, which until two days ago was to his druids. He needed to check on how they were healing. Having a fully capable grove would relieve some of the pressure he was feeling.

Gareth was in the kitchen stirring a pot, which gave off the rich aroma of stew. The warmth of the kitchen and the sight of freshly baked bread awoke Trahaearn's hunger. He broke the end off a warm loaf and spread it with dark honey.

"How are the others?" he asked after swallowing half the bread in one bite. "Is there a chance they will be ready to help?"

Gareth turned from the pot, his gaze on the floor, still unable to look Trahaearn in the eyes. "Two of our brethren may never regain their sanity. The others are healing quickly. Perhaps Dionne could spend some time with them?"

Trahaearn knew that Gareth would have to work out his own feelings about the time he spent in the amulet, and there was no time right now to deal with it even if there was a way. "I'll ask her to see to them when we've finished talking to the other leaders. If she helps the healers first, perhaps that will speed things along. It will be good for you to have help. I thank you for everything you are doing."

"It's not enough, but I will continue to do what I can to keep our grove safe." Gareth turned back to the pot and picked up the spoon.

Trahaearn doubted that cooking would help the druid heal, but didn't comment. Taking the loaf and pot of honey with him, he made his way to the room below where Dionne and Lionel would be almost done creating the circle. They would need sustenance too.

Settling onto the bare earth, Trahaearn sent his power through it to test for weakness. The soil was clean and there was sufficient power for him to restore some of his own depleted energy. The glow was no longer a concern. Humans knew who he was. He worried that the forest folk were a different matter. Humans would be more likely to search harder now that they knew there was magic at the end of it.

When the other two joined him in the center of the circle, Trahaearn sent out a call to the members of the new council. They appeared so quickly he imagined they had been waiting in their own circles.

He told them what had happened so far. There were no questions, which surprised him. "What is happening to the rest of you?"

"The humans have not found Banks' yet," Mark growled.

"Nor have they found the court," Maeve said.

Beacon rubbed his forehead before reporting. The sprite looked worried, and it made Trahaearn wonder if the forest would need a new guardian sooner than expected. If Beacon chose to return to the earth, they would lose a strong and empathetic leader.

"They know we're here, obviously," Beacon said finally. "Now that they know what we are it's getting harder to keep them away. I fear that something is pushing them to find us. If they do, we will have to defend ourselves."

Kali?

"We will do everything we can to keep you safe," Trahaearn promised. "I will send Gareth to you with earth that we'll dig from the roots of the guardian trees. We need less protection than you. The soil will contain the spells to turn people away as the trees do here. It will save you the energy."

"Thanks. It's been hard to keep the folk calm. They're tired... who am I kidding? They are exhausted and angry. The anger doesn't seem to drain them. It seems to power itself."

"It sounds as though Kali has been interfering," Trahaearn said. If she was determined to cause bloodshed, the forest folk were easy targets.

Maeve leaned in as though sharing a secret, even though no one outside the circle could overhear them. "I find myself wondering how much of this is the result of your actions, druid.

You have kicked the hornet's nest rather than calmed the humans."

Trahaearn saw a flash of agreement on Beacon and Mark's faces before they hid their feelings. Dionne and Lionel both shifted position as if coming to his defense. "It may be, but we were never going to get a peaceful solution without some trouble. All we have is a troublesome deity and a lot of anger, surely we should be able to deal with it."

A flash of how Kali would react at his dismissive comment disturbed Trahaearn enough to make him add, "Perhaps Kali is more than troublesome. Do any of you have ideas of how to deal with her?"

Mark shook his head and Trahaearn imagined a small earthquake. Trolls were unfit for subtlety.

"This Angela may be our best hope," Mark rumbled. "Perhaps we can send someone to help her?"

"I am not certain that magical help would sit well with her religious leaders," Trahaearn said. "Let's allow her a little time to find out what she can. Has anyone heard of a deity being... I guess controlled is the wrong word, reasoned with?"

Maeve laughed, a musical trill that warmed Trahaearn. She was turning on the charm and it made him cautious. "The Morrigan is the most reasonable one we have experienced. I did not know her predecessor, but rumor has it that she was not amenable to persuasion. I believe we have to send Kali on her way if we can."

"And what if the next one is worse?" Beacon asked. "We are better off finding a way to work with Kali. Trahaearn may be right; this Angela will find an answer. There will be a way to summon her lover."

As the others argued, Trahaearn reached for more power from the earth beneath him. He'd completed vigils in the past, days of staying awake and seeking enlightenment, but none of those events prepared him for the past two days. He felt every hour, every minute of the time since the prophecy: first the battle to free his druids from the vampires, then dealing with humans. To be fair, his fellow Real Folk were almost as bad as the humans. There had always been friction between the different people in his world. In California, it had been easy to manage around the few fairies and sprites. Here, in Vancouver, there were so many different species of Real Folk and so many in each of the species that the squabbles easily overflowed. Now they were crowded together in hiding, it felt like there was a fuse burning toward a stack of dynamite.

Maeve's voice interrupted his thoughts, "I think we need to start acting on our own interests. If we continue to wait for something to change, we could be massacred."

"It is too soon to be so pessimistic," Trahaearn said. He really wanted to remind her that it was only yesterday they had bullied him into taking charge, but he couldn't trust his tone. If Maeve took offense, he'd lose any authority he held as the representative of the Real Folk.

"When will it be too late?" Mark's rumbling voice cut in before Trahaearn could add anything to make them feel confident.

"I don't know," Trahaearn admitted.

Dionne tapped his knee for permission to talk. When he nodded, she said, "Can we maintain our coalition for a few more days? I believe that Kali is the main barrier between us and the humans. At least we knew there was a deity. The humans believe in all different kinds of gods, and if we can get Kali to be more balanced, there is better chance they will accept her. As it is, they are going to see her as a demon, and probably lump us in with her."

Beacon turned as if listening to an advisor and then spoke, "I am starting to see Maeve's point, but I am told by Queen Bud that we should trust you, druid. I will defend my charges if we are attacked, but otherwise I will hold off for a few more days."

Relief that someone was willing to be patient replaced the draining feeling of failure. "Thank you. I hope it won't come to an attack, but if you can, please minimize the damage during any battle."

The sprite grinned. "It would annoy Kali if there was little bloodshed."

"True, but leave her to us." Trahaearn hoped they would calm Kali before the end of the day tomorrow, that the priests would have an answer for Angela. "We have to keep on our original plan. If we can build an agreement with the humans here, the rest of the world will see it is possible. It will be up to each of us to find a place for our people when we have our agreement, but right now, we need to focus."

"You have until the first human realizes we are here," Mark said. "I will protect this place and I will not worry about the finer points of diplomacy when I do. If Kali feeds from it, then so be it."

Trahaearn relied on the magic that kept Banks' secret. It was the same passive spell as the one on the trees of the grove, and which would soon be in Stanley Park. No glow unless someone had to replenish the power.

"You have two days, druid." Maeve's voice was harsh, or as harsh as a sidhe's voice could be. "I will be preparing my court for battle. A few hundred sidhe warriors will help settle any argument. We will protect this place and will come to the aid of Beacon and Mark if necessary. You may believe we can find a way to live with these people, but I will point out that Kali has been able to influence humans, not Real Folk. If we cannot be victorious, we will die in glory rather than in chains."

Oh, the drama of the sidhe. "I understand, Queen Maeve. Can I ask that you inform us before charging to battle?" Trahaearn couldn't ask her to stop. If things went wrong, an army of sidhe would be needed. He would do his best to avoid things going any more wrong than they already had.

Mark and Beacon said their goodbyes and blinked out of the circle.

"I would speak with you privately, druid." Maeve's words were not a request. "Spell the witch and wizard so they cannot know what I say."

Trahaearn was about to say no, that he trusted and needed Lionel and Dionne, when Lionel answered. "We can leave, Trahaearn. It will only take a moment to open a gate in the circle."

The two rose and Dionne started muttering a spell. Lionel broke the circle in two places, the line of salt between becoming inactive. They stepped across, Dionne casting protections as they did, keeping any creature or spirit from entering. They sealed the circle again and climbed the staircase to the upper floor.

"We are alone," Trahaearn said. "What did you want to say?" Had her threat been bluster for the benefit of the other two council members?

"I want you to know exactly what I plan so you understand I am not issuing empty threats." She held up her hand to silence him. "I have sent two sidhe warriors through the tunnel to Banks' and two who have not conducted magic for days will be leaving to join Beacon in the park. They carry charms that have the power to transport fighters with a word."

"You've given this a great deal of thought," Trahaearn said. If she was this prepared it was even more important to find peace.

"I have. I did not lie when we made this council. I wish for a peaceful outcome. I see many opportunities for the sidhe to prosper in the human world. But I will not allow my people to be slaughtered because we were unprepared. Not even the fairies. They may be distant unwanted relatives of the sidhe court, but they are relatives."

"I understand, Maeve. I will work harder to meet our goals." He had no idea how to work harder than he was, but there must be a way.

"I encourage you to find a solution to Kali. That is the fastest path to resolution either way. As it stands, she is the fastest path to destruction — for both human and Real Folk. Find a way to soften her and she will serve our goal. Imagine humans under the influence of a balanced Kali, if you need encouragement."

Kali as a friend? If she spread peace and cooperation as much as she spread violence, they would be living in harmony with humans before the week was out. "That is an excellent idea, Maeve. Now, if I am to be successful, we need to part. I wish you peace and joy." If wishes could be granted it would be faster than turning Kali, he thought.

KALI WAS DISAPPOINTED IN HER CHOICE OF CHAMPION AND IT was time to put the man in his place. This Jeremiah Nielson had shown great promise at the beginning. He would pay for that lie.

She observed him through the veil before making herself visible, making sure there would be no witnesses to her actions.

He was not alone. She smiled as she recognized the man talking. It was one of the druid's allies; the one she'd spoken to before. The man, his name was not important, he was boring to look at. His hair was brown where it wasn't grey, his skin was pale, his eyes were too. Nothing to attract her, no sparkle, no contrast. Was he attempting to bring her man to their side?

"That was a stupid move," the druid's man said. "If you want to rise in this government, you need to be subtle. The druid is currently popular."

"He must be brought down, Glen," Jeremiah said. "You know that he cannot be allowed to entrench himself in people's hearts. He will become too powerful to destroy."

Kali, realizing that this Glen was playing her kind of game, nudged a little at the man's mind. It was pleasantly devoid of anything other than the need for power, his outward reasonableness simply a tool to achieve his ends.

"I have worked too hard to convince him that I am on his side to let you destroy everything so close to the end," Glen said.

Jeremiah sat down heavily. "You are just playing games. You do this with your friends, your political allies, and your colleagues. God will strike you down. He will not let you use him for your own ends."

"Religion is for sheep," Glen said as he moved to lean over Jeremiah. "I thought you were more... ambitious than that. This announcement, that magic truly exists, is proof of how blind belief can make you stupid. These people can do magic. You witnessed it."

Jeremiah stood suddenly forcing Glen to move back to avoid collision. "Do not deny my belief. You will learn how God reacts in his good time. Tell me how this magic will help you gain power."

Glen turned his back on Jeremiah choosing to stare out of the window. "It will not be long before some fool, magic or not, makes a mistake. I will be the peacemaker. I will rise on the tide of reason."

Jeremiah started laughing. Kali almost struck him dead for the stupidity.

When he gained control of himself, Jeremiah said, "And I suppose that you will make sure something violent will happen? It makes no sense to let your success sit in the hands of fate."

"Whatever it takes," Glen answered.

"What about the vision I had," Jeremiah asked. "The saint?"

Glen turned from the window. "Really? You don't think that was one of these magical folk attempting to sway you? What proof have you that it was a saint?"

"I knew with my heart. I don't need proof." Jeremiah's words were brave, but Kali saw doubt fall over him like a shadow.

She let the conversation fade and withdrew from the room. This Glen was strong minded and able to fool a lot of people about his real motives. She needed someone she could trust to lead her cult. Randall Bluth was as subtle as a hammer and she was learning that more death could be accomplished with more delicate tools.

Glen would make a good high priest. The only problem was he didn't believe, and her first approach had gone so wrong. Perhaps that was because she had come to him in the druid's grove, and when others were present.

She would take a lesson from his style. There would be no demands; there would be no requirement that he worship her. That was a battle she would leave until they had victory in their hands. Men like Randall and Jeremiah were willing to worship, but clearly were not useful in achieving what she needed. Death and pain and destruction on a grand scale needed clear minded planning, not fervent belief.

Yes, Glen would be the right choice.

"You must come," Gareth's words cut through Trahaearn's meditation.

The druid was afraid, and that was unusual enough for Trahaearn to put aside his immediate need to deal with Kali.

"What has happened now?" Trahaearn had no doubt that some calamity had occurred. Gareth would never have interrupted him with just a minor problem.

His druid turned to look down at him from halfway up the stair. "The clearing is full of humans. I do not know how they got past the guardian trees. They are quiet now, but I fear that will not last."

Trahaearn followed Gareth to the front door. It was closed, and a touch confirmed that the spells of protection were still working. The trees might also be still on guard despite the fact that others had found their way to the clearing. Humans were difficult to discourage. If they were determined, they could gather outside the museum, but no amount of determination would get them through the door.

"Any idea what they want?"

Gareth shook his head. "They simply stand as if on vigil. Is it possible that the humans believe they can be trained to become druids?"

Anything was possible. The only way to know for sure was to open the door and speak to the humans. An open door did not mean they would have access, but Trahaearn would ensure the door locked behind him when he stepped forward.

"Where are Lionel and Dionne?" They were probably the most vulnerable people inside the museum. They had survived the battle to regain it from the vampires, but it had been luck more than skill. Neither of them was trained to defend against attack.

"Lionel is in the old section of the library. He mumbled something about finding knowledge in the ancient texts." Gareth's health had returned enough that he could speak in contempt of the wizard.

"Remember what he did to save you." Trahaearn would not let Lionel's sacrifice be forgotten. At least he would be safe among the books. "Dionne?"

"She sleeps in the dormitory. She has exhausted herself attempting to heal our brothers. There is much of the druid in that girl."

Trahaearn didn't argue. Women could not become druids; no matter how many powers they held. If Dionne were destined for a life of study, she would join other groups. "Stand guard over her. I will go and speak to these humans."

Gareth paused as if to argue, but after a moment's reflection, he nodded and retreated to the stairs leading to the dormitory.

Alone, Trahaearn thought through what he was about to do. If these humans were friendly, it would be a matter of minutes to ascertain their purpose and deal with it. If they were not, and that was most likely from Trahaearn's experience, then he would leave them to the clearing. It was not worth his energy to try to persuade them when he needed to make the world safe from Kali.

He opened the door and stepped through before anyone noticed.

The crowd was all human, but a few more women were standing among the men than earlier. The door shut at a silent command, and Trahaearn noticed a brightening of his skin. It seemed that it took less magic to start the glow now than it had at first.

The quiet click of the lock caught the attention of the closest humans. They turned to look at him, the rest of the crowd reacting at the same time, as if there was only one mind driving the bodies. This was not a friendly crowd.

"What is your purpose here?" Trahaearn made his voice carry across the clearing.

One man stood forward, eyes bright. "Kali commanded us."

Others in the crowd started to chant *Kali, Kali*.

Trahaearn kept his focus on the man who spoke. "And what does Kali want with this place?"

"We are her eyes and heart." His words echoed by the mass of humans. Almost all of them joined the original chanters.

As he observed the people, Trahaearn realized that Kali's influence traveled like an infection. A few individuals turned into true believers passed the disease onto others.

No. She is a power; I must stop thinking of her as something to be cured.

"As her eyes, do you know who attacked the magical folk in the park?" It was worth a try to engage them, maybe break the connection with Kali.

The man didn't respond. Trahaearn looked more closely. The human was empty of any thought. He was a puppet and the same was happening to the people around him. Perhaps Kali wasn't interested in followers, she simply needed tools.

He wasn't going to get any information from the crowd, and he wasn't willing to stand and watch as the humans became empty shells as Kali's power burned them from the inside out. It was time to return to the museum and start repairing the damage.

Perhaps these few were lost, but others could be saved.

. . .

KALI THINNED THE VEIL TO SEE WHAT HER FOLLOWERS WERE doing. The mob at the druid's museum was keeping him inside. That would stop him from calming the world down, but it was a standoff not a victory. It wouldn't generate the death and pain she needed. It was time to gather the new leader to her side. The man, Glen, would be much better than the fool she trusted to kill Trahaearn. Randall Bluth might be an agent of chaos, but he wasn't capable of completing a task. And now the humans had him incarcerated. It would be a small matter to remove Bluth from their flimsy jail, and she would. A little chaos was a good thing as long as she didn't rely on it alone to achieve the bloodshed she envisioned.

She pressed against the veil, feeling for Glen's presence. The veil connected to every point on the human plane. With one touch, she could summon the essence of any being on that world. She was hungry. It was unfortunate that she couldn't feed on the essence of the living. It was heartening to know that there were more than simply the rich powers of death that would sustain her if all she craved was sustenance, there was always sex.

Glen was in his office.

Kali considered how to appear. In her own form, she was an object to fear. The man may not listen if she appeared to him in her real radiance. Would he listen if she was merely a voice?

It troubled Kali that she could not simply do as she pleased. She calmed her simmering anger with the thought of the future. A time when she could march across the human plane with no disguise, trampling beings under her feet, feeding constantly. Becoming stronger and more magnificent with each step.

"Glen," she called in a voice tempered to a sweet and seductive tone.

He looked up from his papers. Kali paused for a moment to assess his expression. There was no concern, no fear. The man seemed unfazed by a disembodied voice calling his name. Perhaps the druid had done her a favor by making him accustomed to the mystical.

He turned his head trying to locate the source of the words. "Who are you?"

She stayed behind the veil. "I am Kali."

"Why do you not show yourself as you did before?"

The man would have to learn the proper attitude, but for now a little arrogance would serve. She would use it to twist him to her ends. Had he known she was there in Jeremiah's study? When had he seen her? It was another troubling thought that she had forgotten the man. It must have been in the first hours of her ascendancy. There were moments at the beginning that faded behind the hunger that had consumed her.

Kali slipped through the veil and stood waiting for him to worship her.

He simply stared at her, and she fought the urge to smite him. His mind was locked, and he would need training. She knew he would not allow fear to cloud his actions. He would complete his tasks as she required.

"I did not wish to startle you," she said.

"I am not easily startled."

She saw him try to casually return to the papers on his desk. He wanted her to think he was unaffected, but he could not make himself turn away. She had cast no command on his body, the inability was from within himself.

Kali watched, curious to know how he would end this struggle. She smiled when Glen grimaced as if impatient and ceased to fight against his urges.

"What do you want from me?" He still managed that unseemly attitude.

His words drew the memory from the haze of her early days. The first time she had answered that question, it was an order to kill Trahaearn. This mortal had denied her then. Fury burned through Kali fast and hot. She was gratified to see fear cross Glen's face. This time he would obey her, or she would take his life.

"I have believers who need a leader. I want you to be that leader."

The ambition in the man's eyes told Kali that she'd found the right bait.

"I don't believe in gods." The words lacked conviction.

"Do you deny that I am a goddess?"

"I do not know what you are. But you seem powerful. Will I be powerful if I align with you?"

Kali felt the wave of greed flowing from Glen. He desperately wanted her to convince him.

"Yes." She sent the word out on a wave of power, something she wouldn't be able to do often until blood ran in the streets. She imbued that single word with a command to believe. If the man were truly ready, he would be hers.

The battle in Glen's mind between his desire for power and his belief was almost enough to sustain Kali. It wasn't a bodily death. It was a spiritual one. The energy was sweet, but insubstantial.

Greed for power won. "I will do what you want."

"I want the druid stopped."

"Then we should discuss the best way to do that." Glen gestured to a chair as if she was a mortal being who had come to visit. She would enjoy teaching him the proper way to worship a goddess when she was finished with him.

"I do not require rest," she said. "How do you intend to get my worshipers to kill the druid?"

Glen smiled and the gleam of greed returned to his eyes.

❧ 14 ❧

This was the longest three days in Trahaearn's life, and it was only halfway through the third. It felt as though every time he had a plan, or even a hint of progress, something else hit him back.

The mob sitting outside was no problem, yet. They chanted and that might be annoying, but it wasn't violent. Angela was still meeting with her priests, and Glen was out of communication. Jacob was working on getting a meeting with the right people — whoever they were. He mentioned a premier, and a prime minister, they seemed to be the same position, but Dionne assured Trahaearn that they were not.

The President of The United States and other heads of state throughout the world were flying in. If he could get them together, he could lay out his plans. Well, not plans, more a vision. That was if he could do it without attracting Kali to the meeting. He didn't want to think about what she would do to create her own dream of the future.

The thought of all these problems was overwhelming. Trahaearn needed a success. Even if it was small, he needed to achieve something. He strode into the lab where they had battled the vampires. It was still a mess, but perhaps cleaning a bit of the debris would be that little step forward he needed to lift his mood.

"Quinn Larson is requesting entrance," Gareth said from the broken door to the lab. "Also, Markel has recovered sufficiently to take the healing duties from Dionne if you need her."

Trahaearn told Gareth to let Quinn enter and join him in the kitchen. He would take Markel's recovery as his small victory. Dionne may want to continue her work there, but she would be more useful at his side when he dealt with — no, that was too aggressive — met with the humans. They all seemed more willing to be cooperative with a pretty girl in attendance. And Dionne had a sharp mind, which could disarm them.

In the kitchen, he poured black tea for himself and offered a mug to Quinn. "What brings you here? Please tell me nothing more has gone wrong."

Quinn settled on the bench that ran the length of the main table. "No, or not yet. I don't think we can expect to have an easy path. Kali isn't just acting for her own desires. I have a theory that she is here because she is a reflection of the world as it stands."

That was interesting. Perhaps it would give an answer to the problem she posed. "So if we can change the world, she will change. Or she will go?"

Quinn laughed. "It is only a theory. I don't know if you feel it, but it's like there's a balance right now. That everything is motionless and must start moving again or we die. Something will turn that stillness to action. The balance will tip to one side or the other soon. Kali represents the other side."

As much as he wanted to dive into a discussion about this theory, Trahaearn knew they didn't have time. The problem of Kali was in Angela's hands right now. If she was unable to solve it, perhaps they had time to explore Quinn's idea.

"Was that the reason for your visit?"

"No. I have news." He looked up toward the ground as though he was assessing the activity outside the museum. "I wouldn't have come through that cult upstairs just for a chat."

"I can send you back through the tunnel."

Quinn looked puzzled. "I thought the front door was the only way in or out."

"No. We would not allow ourselves to be trapped in here. But it's good that everyone else thinks that."

"I'll keep the secret," Quinn assured him. "So, my news. We have discovered the identity of the human who set fire to the forest." He held up his hand and an image appeared above his palm.

"He's the one who tried to kill me after the press conference." Trahaearn leaned in, but there was nothing else about the image that he could use. "How do you know?"

"We found some pixies hiding in the roots of one of the old trees. They were weak and their glows were almost extinguished. They produced the image."

"Are they well now?" Trahaearn didn't want to hear that more Real Folk had died, but he needed the truth.

"They are with Beacon and healthy. What are we going to do?"

"The man is in jail at the moment. We can let the human authorities know what he has done. I can give them the image, but I don't know what they will be able to do with it. I would guess their laws do not anticipate the use of magic as proof in court."

Quinn drained his cup and then looked around the kitchen. They were alone, but he leaned inward so they could speak quietly. "I have other news. It's no more than a feeling, a few whispers that were cut off as I got close, but I think Maeve is planning something."

So, this was the cost of his small victory. "What do you think it is?" Perhaps it was simply confirmation of what she'd already told him.

"I was in Banks'. The sidhe are moving through the tunnel between the court and the bar. They are taking others through to the court. Mark says they've been doing it since the change."

Troubling. This was far more than he anticipated from her warning.

"Do these others come back?"

"Some. But it's not pixies and fairies they are taking. It's kobolds and folk like that."

Trahaearn rubbed his temples. The sidhe were collecting Real Folk who knew how to fight. "Maeve said she had plans, but she wasn't up front with the real details. Now I know it was more than the usual sidhe machinations. She's planning war. Do you think Kali has influenced her?"

Quinn shrugged. "I doubt it. You know Maeve. She's always got something up her sleeve. She has plan A, B, and Z. I think she's preparing her defenses not getting ready to be the first to fight. You have time, not much, but you do have some time."

"Maeve isn't the only one with a deadline. If we don't get this worked out in the next couple of days, I fear we will have lost without even calling for battle." He couldn't do anything about the sidhe queen. Even if he confronted her, she'd have a story to divert him. She'd lie if his questions offended her.

It was a good reminder that all of his problems weren't human.

"I'd like to visit with Dionne and Lionel before I go." Quinn looked around again. "Are they here?"

Trahaearn was about to direct Quinn when Dionne ran into the room.

"That nutcase who attacked you escaped from jail!"

"Get Lionel," Trahaearn said. The man must be caught. He would be an impediment to peace. If they had to worry about attack, or begin guarding against it, there would be no chance for trust between the humans and the magical folk. The only solution was to search for this man and make sure he was returned to the authorities. Whether he was working on Kali's command, or acting on his own, he was dangerous.

Quinn sat waiting for Dionne to leave before saying, "You don't need to order her around. She's not an apprentice. What are you planning?"

Trahaearn didn't argue or apologize for his tone with Dionne. He knew that she was capable of telling him if she didn't like the way he spoke to her. Although, he rarely issued orders, so it was a sign of how frustrated he was with the world. "We need to find this man before he does irreparable damage. The others don't trust the humans. If he burns the park down, or kills one of the Real Folk, I fear we will never be able to live among the humans."

"It's probably a good thing that they underestimate our abilities. If they knew how powerful we were, there would be enough bloodshed for two Kalis," Quinn said, giving voice to Trahaearn's fears.

Lionel and Dionne joined them in the kitchen, ending any further discussion on the possible repercussions. Trahaearn asked them to stand in the corner, where there was less light. Both glowed, but it was muted. They would be safe in the daylight, but this search wasn't necessarily going to stay in the light. "Make sure you both have defensive charms. Nothing fatal, but I don't want you getting hurt."

Quinn dug into the pockets of his coat and drew out a handful of the nuts, shells, and seeds that he used to hold his charms. "Here, take these. I can make more. They'll cause confusion, or distraction. I have nothing that will act as a weapon." He explained the specific purpose of each to Dionne. When he was done, he stood with them, clearly signaling that Lionel and Dionne were his responsibility.

Trahaearn didn't respond to the message. If they had any real problems, they'd work it out after the world was set to rights. "We're going through the tunnel. I won't make you take an oath, but I will ask that you keep our secret. This exit is our only option while the cult occupies the clearing."

He led them to the back of the small room he used as an office, and through the narrow space to where Dionne had hidden the day they proved the magic to Jacob. It felt like years had passed, but it was only days. Reaching up to the mark on the brick that would reveal the door to the tunnel, a moment's doubt flashed through Trahaearn's mind. What if this museum was different? In his haste to act, he hadn't thought to confirm the location of the tunnel.

Relief flooded him as his fingers found the thin lines of the rune. He was too emotional. He needed to get himself under control.

The door appeared as an outline of silvery light and then the bricks all disappeared to reveal the steps that would lead them below the museum and out into the forest behind the cult members. When they were through, the door reformed and they were left with only the glows from magic to light their way.

Trahaearn spelled a light to float in front of them so they wouldn't find themselves stumbling as the glows faded. He used the journey through the passage to calm his mind. No one spoke while they traveled. Perhaps they were all doing the same.

When they reached the end, Trahaearn doused the light and looked at his companions in the remaining glow from Lionel and Dionne's skin. Quinn was pale and there was a sheen of sweat on his face. "Are you ill?"

The wizard shook his head. "The last time I was underground I went blind. I'll be fine when we get out of here."

"When I open the door, go through quickly. I'll send a seeker spell as soon as the door is closed. If we have any luck due to us, we'll find the man fast and get back inside before anyone knows we're out."

At their nods, he reached for the rune that would open the tunnel. Daylight shone green through the canopy of trees. There was no one in sight, but the chanting from the clearing was audible. They were only a few yards away from the cult.

Leaning against the nearest tree, Trahaearn summoned the power he needed from the earth. He visualized the man who had attacked him and asked the spirit of the soil to guide them. A tug at this chest confirmed that the spirit agreed.

Given the way their luck was going, it didn't surprise Trahaearn that the tug pulled him toward the clearing, and the Kali mob.

⚜ 15 ⚜

The druid was out of the museum.

Kali felt a tug of recognition before she saw the man she wanted to influence. An interesting new development. Up to now she'd only been able to recognize people when she saw them. Would she eventually feel this with everyone she needed? That would become wearing. And it would probably be a useless asset because feeling everyone would drown out the people she wanted to locate.

Putting aside the thoughts, she reached for Bluth's mind. While Glen was preparing himself to be her representative, she would use the tools she had.

The human was still boiling with rage inside. She'd lifted him from his prison to let him cause mayhem. The mob was not acting violently enough for her needs. Bluth should have whipped them up, but he'd just arrived. Now she would use him to stop the druid.

"Your enemy is in the trees," she whispered in his ear. "Find him and destroy him."

His eyes filled with a hunger for blood that was a poor reflection of her own but would do. She used a thread of power to guide him toward the druid and his companions. With Trahaearn dead, perhaps the museum doors would open.

Four people stood together beside a large oak. The trees were dense enough to dim the sunlight with their canopy. Trahaearn was looking directly toward Bluth.

The druid had used magic; she could tell by the glow that lit the trees around him.

"Stop," Trahaearn commanded Bluth.

A flash of power revealed his spell to her as it flew toward Bluth.

The man was frozen in place.

Kali probed the magic looking for a way to undo it.

"Refuse his command," she ordered. The spell would untangle, but she needed Bluth to fight it with her.

The man's mind was so twisted that she couldn't tell if he heard her command, or if he was simply enraged by the spell that held him. He struggled to raise his arm. She could see the words form in his mind as he fought to speak.

"Do not use your evil power on me, wizard." The words seemed to release a little of the spell holding him.

Kali stepped through the veil and stood behind her worshipper. Being on the same plane made it easier for her to reach into the spell. She ripped it from around Bluth and shoved him forward before retreating back through the veil.

"Die," Bluth screamed as he ran arms extended grasping for Trahaearn's throat.

The girl with them tossed a handful of seeds between the druid and the human. The air filled with black motes that clouded around Bluth.

Kali reached for his mind and heard the buzzing and chattering that was disrupting his concentration. She nullified the charm with a thought.

Her powers were growing.

Bluth started his charge again, single-minded rage fueling his actions. Whatever happened next, the man would be burned to a shell inside. Kali would show him mercy by taking his life when he killed the druid.

"Kali, you cannot win." The druid seemed to look right at her.

Could he see through the veil?

No, Kali decided it was simply a coincidence. She chose not to respond. Let the druid wonder if he was wrong.

The older wizard with Trahaearn tossed another charm. This one turned into a rope that tangled around Bluth's feet. The man's momentum brought him crashing to the ground. His head connected with a tree root and he blacked out.

Kali tried to wake him, learning too late that she needed a conscious mind to control someone. The druid moved fast.

She couldn't rouse Bluth quickly enough to counter him. This time there was no magic. He took a rope from a bag and tied Bluth securely, arms, feet, and legs.

"I know you are there, Kali," the druid said. "We will not kill this man. You have damaged him severely, but perhaps we can heal him. If not, humans will have him back as he is. It is possible they can succeed where we fail."

His arrogance burned her.

She slipped through the veil to confront him. "What I have done cannot be healed, druid. Do not assume you are powerful enough to undo my efforts. Killing this man would be a kindness. One I am not of a mind to do. No matter, I can turn others to my uses. This man is not important enough to get in my way. You are naïve if you think that I have not already turned others."

Why had she said that? Glen must be a secret until she decided it was time. His betrayal must be handled delicately to get the most effect.

Trahaearn didn't flinch at her rage. "You may be able to turn the humans, but we will fight for them. We will not allow you to win."

His denial of her power weakened her. It felt like a tap had opened in her being. The energy that had been powering her from Bluth's rage was gone. She needed to feed and could not allow these fools to see her weakness. She laughed and faded beyond the veil where she could see bright pools of death and pain to assuage her hunger. It would take no time at all to sate herself and then return to defeat this druid.

She listened for what they would do next before leaving for her banquet of agony.

"Let's get him into the tunnel."

The druid had another entrance. They would not be successful. Before she fed, Kali would send her mob to stall her enemies.

Trahaearn bent to drag Bluth toward the entrance to the tunnel. Inside they could cast a spell to get him back to the museum. When they were safe, he'd ask Dionne to try healing him. Markel would help. If they could heal the man's mind, perhaps his link to Kali could be severed. Finding a way to release people from her thrall would be a step toward getting rid of her.

"Hurry," Quinn's voice cut through Trahaearn's thoughts.

The sounds of shouting and running feet hit him as he turned to look behind. The mob from the clearing was coming. By the noise, it was all of them. The tunnel was too far away to save them.

"Dionne, Lionel, do you have any charms to help?" Knowing they wouldn't reach the tunnel in time didn't prevent him from dragging the body toward it.

"Nothing that will work on that many people," Quinn answered for them. "We will have to fight."

It was getting harder to avoid doing as Kali wanted. The more followers she gathered, the easier it was for her to push a situation to the edge of violence. He could hear her laugh, and worried that it was not just his imagination and frustration fueling the sound.

"No one dies," he said as he laid Bluth against a tree. The man showed no signs of waking. At least he couldn't help stoke the violence that was coming. "If we can stun them, Kali won't be able to push them to kill us."

Quinn stood next to the unconscious man. "We can't hope for them all to trip and hit their heads. I have, maybe, a dozen charms that will drop people into sleep. Dionne, might be able to stun them with a touch, but she'll run out of energy before the crowd is done."

Lionel moved to stand beside Dionne. "I have some distraction charms. Perhaps the ones on the periphery will be more susceptible. I can protect Dionne for a while."

The shouts and footfalls were almost upon them. "If it comes to it, run. Let the mob have Bluth back." Trahaearn glanced behind. "The tunnel will not stay open for long, perhaps ten more minutes. If you run now, you can make it."

Dionne stepped forward. "Only if you come. We can leave Bluth, but if you stay alone, or even you and Quinn, you won't survive. Those people are coming to kill you. If you won't fight back, they will win."

He felt a simple gladness that they weren't going to abandon him, it was tempered with fear that they would be foolish. Trahaearn couldn't let anyone be killed. "I don't know what will happen if they get here and we are gone."

Quinn moved away from the unconscious man. "We fight as best we can then. Is there any way to call your druids?"

"Yes, but two more people won't make a difference."

The first of the mob broke past the trees before he could decide what to do. Instinctively Trahaearn tossed a barrier spell. It held, but bent toward them under the strain of bodies. "Run for the tunnel. I'll be right behind."

He held the barrier long enough to see that they had obeyed, running along different paths toward safety. It would be hard for the mob to catch them. When his companions were past the closest trees, Trahaearn stopped feeding energy to the barrier. He had one spell that would save him, one that would only work for a druid. Reaching deep into the earth, he found the spirit and called for its aid.

The first hands reached for him as the ground opened around his feet and he sank into the earth.

THE SCREAMS OF FURY AT HIS DISAPPEARANCE FILTERED through the two feet of earth above his head. The spirit had pulled him only as far as needed. The bubble of air around his head would keep him alive for up to an hour, but Trahaearn would only stay enclosed in the soil until he was sure that the mob had left.

As he waited, Trahaearn felt the vibrations of the mob's movements shift away. He thought it was toward the museum clearing, but any sense of direction was hard to hang onto inside the earth. He felt their steps long after the shouts and screams died off. He could sense that the air in his bubble was becoming stale; it had probably been a half hour since he sank below the surface — much longer than he wanted.

Trahaearn began the movement that would send him back to the surface as soon as the last set of feet left the clearing. He rose in a defensive stance, arms free and raised to his shoulders to protect his face. He would not kill, but a well-placed punch would likely save his life as much as a spell.

There was no one in sight.

He relaxed his stance and looked around. Bluth's body was in pieces. The mob had ripped his arms from his body, his legs were still attached but lay twisted. The violence was beyond Trahaearn's experience. The humans had been mindless, must have been to do this much damage to a fellow being. The fact that Bluth was unconscious while it was happening, may have been a kindness.

Dusting the last of the soil from his clothes, Trahaearn headed for the tunnel. They had no more time. This situation had to be resolved, and they needed to be ready when the world leaders arrived. He would contact Jacob as soon as he got back.

The tunnel door opened as soon as he pressed the rune on the tree trunk. The rune was fresh, and that meant Gareth had been doing more than simply taking care of the other druids.

He ran the distance to the museum as soon as the door was secure behind him. Even in his eagerness, Trahaearn wasn't willing to risk anyone finding an entrance to the museum.

Quinn was waiting for him on the other side of the tunnel. The wizard stopped mid-pace. "Where are Dionne and Lionel?"

16

"They are not here?"

Trahaearn felt foolish as soon as the words were out. Quinn would not have asked if they were. "When you split up? I saw them run together to the left. They should have met you at the tunnel or been right behind you."

Quinn shook his head. "They never reached the tunnel. I waited inside the entrance for them. When the door closed, they were still out there. I tried to leave, but that door closes fast." He hurried toward the stairs. "We have to find them."

Trahaearn followed Quinn to the front hall. If the mob had returned to the clearing, they wouldn't get far. "We need to go back through the tunnel. It won't help them if we are torn apart, Quinn. The mob is no longer satisfied with a little chanting."

He reached for Quinn's arm to stop his headlong rush to leave. As he connected, someone pounded on the door. Was it Jacob? The crowd outside must not have connected Jacob with the druids. It wouldn't be long until they did, and then his passage would become too dangerous. "Wait here." He threw a command spell in his voice. There would be repercussions from Quinn, but Trahaearn could only handle one crisis at a time.

The only way to know who was demanding attention was to open the door and that was too dangerous. No matter what resulted from his efforts to create a safe future, all of the museums would need a spell to identify callers from now forward. Humans could not send a spell asking permission and the druids could not be at anyone's beck and call.

If only wishes were real, he thought. He'd wish that there was no threat outside. But wishes were only fulfilled by magic, and no magic could really change what was happening. Trahaearn pushed aside the useless thoughts and opened the door.

Instead of Jacob with plans to meet the leaders of all the humans, the fool from the press conference was standing on the threshold. He had his own camera people.

"What can I do for you?" Trahaearn asked, trying to be polite and yet not waste the time that they could use looking for Lionel and Dionne.

"I am the Reverend Jeremiah Nielson, and I am here to save the souls of those who have strayed from the true path."

The man took a step forward to enter the museum as if he didn't expect to need an invitation. He ran face first into the barrier spell that remained in place until Trahaearn was willing to release it. Until today, Trahaearn would have released it as part of the door opening. Any druid opening a door would say the words that allowed a visitor to enter. Until recently, the door was left open — although, Trahaearn reflected, the vampires may not have been as willing to let people enter as real druids were.

"You may do as you wish outside these walls," Trahaearn responded. "Those within have no need of your services." He reached to push the door closed but Nielson held something out to him, a small tablet that had images flowing across.

"Are you afraid that they will feel differently when they see this?" Nielson tried to force the tablet through the barrier.

Trahaearn looked at the images. It was a film of Bluth's murder, of the mob in frenzied action. He looked over the crowd behind Nielson, it didn't take magic to identify the perpetrators of the horror on the screen.

"No. Why would I fear that?"

"You caused this," Nielson said, his voice projecting to the mob.

The man had trapped him in a conversation that would only delay the search. Trahaearn watched as the members of the mob seemed to lean forward for an answer. There was nothing he could say that wouldn't play to Kali's hands. "That is not correct," he stated. His tone meant to end the conversation. He pushed the door closed on Nielson's face.

He turned back to see Quinn struggling against the command spell.

"You are free to move." He waited for the anger in the wizard's eyes to turn into a reprimand, but it faded away.

"This is getting out of hand," Quinn said. "Let's get to the tunnel."

It has been out of hand since the prophecy came to be.

Better to focus on what they could control at least until they could solve the bigger problems. "Would they go somewhere? Dionne and Lionel? If they couldn't make it to the tunnel?"

"Banks' is a long way to run. My house is almost as far." Quinn raced for the entrance to the tunnel. "They'd go to ground, but you and I know that they aren't hiding. Someone has them."

Trahaearn didn't think Kali had the subtly yet to take hostages. If the mob had Lionel and Dionne, it was likely that they were dead — if not now, then soon. The thought tore at his heart.

"We'll send a locator spell. If it is simply that the humans have them, no one will be blocking us with magic." He pressed the rune to open the doorway.

"Arch Druid, you have a visitor," Gareth's voice stopped them from entering the tunnel.

Trahaearn turned to meet Gareth.

"No," Quinn said. "Tell me how to open the other end. I'll search by myself."

Placing his hand on Quinn's arm, Trahaearn said, "It is too dangerous to go alone. Gareth would not have stopped us if this visitor were unimportant. A few minutes to see who it is, and then I promise we will go."

He couldn't use another command spell, and if Quinn insisted, he'd provide the information that would open the other door. It would only be a matter of a few moments to change the words needed after Quinn was gone.

Quinn looked down the passage as though hoping to see his friends. His shoulders slumped.

"A few moments," he said. "I will come with you, so I can make up my own mind whether this visitor merits us delaying."

Jacob was waiting for them in the front hall. "We need to show them this," he said without preamble.

Trahaearn ached to rescue Lionel and Dionne, but he reached for the tablet that Jacob held out. It showed the same action as Nielson's. Trahaearn watched until the point where Nielson's film ended. This one continued.

It showed his own spell drawing him into the earth, and then the murder of Bluth. When the mob couldn't work out their rage on Trahaearn, they swarmed the unconscious body, and started tearing at his clothes. The movie camera remained steady as the mob continued, when Bluth was naked, they started tearing at his skin, then his limbs until the man's arms were scattered around the trees. When there was no more of his bloody flesh to tear, the crowd suddenly lost their rage. Bodies slumping, they turned toward the museum and shuffled off.

"Kali must have enjoyed that," Quinn said. "She'll be well fed and ready for the next horror."

Trahaearn nodded. "Who took this?" He didn't ask why the person hadn't intervened; he'd done the same, stayed hidden until sure of survival. No one person could have made a difference.

Jacob reached for the tablet. "No one knows. It was posted on the web. We have to show this to that guy Nielson. He's trying to make it your fault. He's edited the video and if he gets any traction, no one will care what the real show was." He reached for the door handle, but when he tried to turn it, nothing happened. "What the hell?"

Trahaearn touched Jacob's arm. "I need to know how you got through that crowd." If Jacob had come through unharmed, there was hope for Lionel and Dionne.

"There's only a few people there and I don't think they were part of the riot." He pointed to the door. "We have to get that TV crew to check the real video out."

The fact that the mob had dispersed so quickly was probably not a good thing. At least while they were occupying his front lawn, they were not on a murderous rampage. "Do you really need me for this? We have our own crisis to deal with."

"It would be better if you could answer some questions. But I get it. You have the world to save, right?" The sarcasm in his tone left no doubt as to Jacob's feelings. "Your image is part of saving the world. At least come out and show them your face. I'll cut off any questions."

Trahaearn looked back to where Quinn was standing. "I will only be a few minutes." He didn't wait for an answer. The wizard had nowhere to go.

He touched the door and cleared the spell. Outside it was just as Jacob had said. There were a few people at the edge of the trees. They had tents pitched and were gathering dead branches to build a fire. One of the women saw Trahaearn step out. She called to her companions and they started applauding and cheering.

"See you have your own cult, Trahaearn," Jacob said.

Trahaearn ignored the comment. He was not interested in a cult. His thirteen druids were all the followers he needed.

Nielson was still standing facing the door. He'd at least had the sense to step back from the threshold. The man was probably waiting to ambush Jacob.

"Come here," Trahaearn commanded. He would not allow Nielson any power in this. It was not an interview. When the lone remaining cameraman followed, Trahaearn motioned for Jacob to begin.

He stood straight and spoke to the camera. "Jeremiah Nielson came here to accuse the Arch Druid of inciting a riot, to blame him for the murder of Randall Bluth, a mentally ill man. He used false evidence. Here is the real proof of the murder."

Jacob held the tablet straight out and the cameraman focused on the film that was playing.

Trahaearn was impressed when Jacob spoke over the carnage. "This act of violence has nothing to do with the magical people in our midst. They only want peace and to live alongside us." He pointed at the screen of his tablet. "This murder is the action of a mindless mob, and every one of them is human."

The cameraman asked Jacob something, and they exchanged cards. Then he turned off his camera and looked at Nielson. "Don't try to get me involved in something like this again. I have my reputation to protect. If you need to keep going, I'm sure the paparazzi will help." The cameraman strode off, putting his equipment away as he crossed the clearing.

Before Nielson could react, Trahaearn pulled Jacob through the door and then closed it.

"We must go now, Jacob," Trahaearn said. He didn't want to tell the man why. If anyone knew that Lionel and Dionne were missing, it could cause more violence.

"Okay, but you need to be ready for the heads of state tomorrow. I'll arrange for someone to get you to the meeting after all the security people are satisfied that no one will get assassinated." He dug into his pocket and brought out a phone. "Keep it, and I'll call you. I get the feeling it's not going to be safe to come here for a while."

Frustrated that not knowing where Kali's cult had gone did make it dangerous for his allies, Trahaearn looked at the phone and frowned.

Jacob reached for it and opened it like a clamshell. "It will ring, and you just open it. When the call is finished, you close it."

"Thank you," Trahaearn said. "I think it's safe for you to go through the clearing now, but if you need to see me, phone first. I have other ways if the front door is no longer available."

SATED FROM THE VIOLENCE AT THE DRUID'S HOME, KALI floated behind the veil. Things were moving well; her followers were more than capable of mindless destruction. Now she would be kept strong enough to plan bloodshed that would sustain her for centuries.

There was a lingering taste of agony in the clearing that she wanted to savor. Slipping through the veil, she touched her flesh to the blood-soaked soil. It was delicious.

"Kali?"

The word startled her, but she had enough control to hide it. Who would have the audacity to speak to her before receiving permission? She turned to see the fool Jeremiah Nielson staring at her. How had he known it was her? He had only seen her in her meek disguise.

"I know it's you. Glen told me what you really look like. I know you are not a saint, but I believe you to be more godly than these magical creatures who are poised to destroy everything good in the world."

You have no idea what I am capable of.

Well, if he had one use it was to amuse her. She smiled at him, but he flinched. "You are still willing to assist me?"

"If it will rid us of this plague, yes. I believe I can help you and still be right with God. Perhaps I can show you the way to his side?"

Kali smothered the laugh. If his god existed, he was in hiding like the others. "What if I need you to kill someone?" If this man were willing to do what it took, she would drain his good intentions and then destroy him. It warmed her to know that humans would prefer to follow her, rather than believe that their myths had power.

"It is against my faith to kill. I cannot believe that is the only way to serve your needs."

That was the only way to feed her. Kali fought the urge to tell Jeremiah Nielson that death was the only end; the manner of death was the difference. "The people who would oppose me must be removed. They will not change."

"And, if I do this one thing, what will become of me? Of my soul?"

The words didn't sound like a plea. He was negotiating. The knowledge of his real motives was almost as sweet as the remnants of Bluth's death.

"Is that the most important thing to you? Is your god only worthy of worship if he can make your life better?"

The man squirmed. "The promise of heaven is enough." The lies sang in his voice. "Is that what you offer? Heaven?"

Tired of the exchange, and disappointed that Nielson was so weak as to think she would treat him any differently than the other humans, Kali stood taller. "No. I offer you the chance to do my bidding. If that is not sufficient, then I have no use for you. There are millions of others who would adore me without expecting reward."

At least Glen knew the value of power, even if it was fleeting. It would not be enough to satisfy him, she knew, but Glen would kill many before she discarded him. This one was simply an annoyance.

Nielson's face contorted with rage that seemed to fill him and overflow into the world. "You promised me a reward when you came to me, Kali."

Kali saw the emotion as it flooded the man's entire being, a blush of red that intensified to burn like a sun. It was such a waste. This much rage would have worked in her favor, but it had no depth, there was nothing in it to sustain her.

"I have decided that I do not wish to reward you." She started to slip through the veil. "I have no need of you now."

Standing halfway between this world and the one beyond the veil, Kali had little power in either, but she wanted to watch as he realized his mistake. Would he beg? That would be amusing.

The glow of fury in Jeremiah's being faded into a coldness that seemed to suck energy from Kali.

"You will regret this," he said. "You cannot treat me this way."

Kali laughed as she slipped beyond the veil.

You will not live long enough to exact revenge.

The man was a child.

17

Trahaearn stood with Quinn on the step in front of the museum door. The feeling of peace had returned. The mob no longer overwhelmed the calming spell that was soaked deep into the soil of the clearing. The few people who were still there sat together, the murmuring of their conversation adding to the serenity. Trahaearn tried to ignore their occasional glances.

"We should start our search before something else gets in the way," he said.

Quinn was casting a location spell, keeping himself hidden from the humans by using Trahaearn as a shield. "The spell will be done in a moment. They have both been here too often for it to find their most recent path easily."

The wizard didn't look up from the twigs in his hand. He was using the spell that Lionel had created, the one that found the amulet.

"Will it work if they are separated?" Trahaearn asked as the twigs continued to spin in Quinn's hand.

"I've asked it to locate Dionne," Quinn answered. "She is the most vulnerable."

That might not be true, but Trahaearn chose not to argue. Both of them were young for wizards. Lionel may be more used to the world of magical folk, but Dionne knew humans. And they could both fight. "It's not working."

Quinn closed his hand and glared at Trahaearn. "I don't need you to point out the obvious. We have to go back to where we were separated. There are too many paths here. Is the tunnel faster?"

"No. You didn't notice, but it wanders a bit. Follow me." Trahaearn marched toward the edge of the trees.

As they approached the edge of the tree line, one of the humans ran to join them. It was a young woman, eagerness shining in her eyes.

"Can we help?"

I don't need this!

"No. Thank you for offering. Please stay as long as you wish." Quinn was already past the first line of trees. "We must go."

Trahaearn didn't wait for her response. Hurrying after the wizard, he grabbed his arm. "This way," he said, pulling Quinn to the left.

"You shouldn't encourage them," Quinn said. "They will bring trouble."

He couldn't blame Quinn. The wizard had no evidence that humans could be kind. His experience was limited to the woman who kept bothering him about Dionne's wellbeing before the prophecy, and Dionne who could be as difficult to manage as any apprentice.

"We cannot afford to alienate anyone who isn't afraid of us." He changed direction again to avoid a tangle of brambles.

"Until I have Dionne and Lionel safely at my side, I plan to treat every human as a threat."

Trahaearn stopped walking. He turned and held up his hand to stall Quinn. "That's feeding the problem. Are you going to attack every human we see?" He couldn't believe that Quinn, who'd fought the vampires alongside him, and tried to save them despite the damage they'd done, would change so much.

Quinn took in a deep breath and seemed to think the question over. When he looked up at Trahaearn again, there was an unfamiliar hardness in his eyes. "I won't attack, but I will defend with all of my power. This truce you are trying to forge is no good if the humans don't want it."

Trahaearn stood firm as Quinn tried to push his way past. This was not his truce. If Quinn really felt this way, then the others of the council would soon be taking their own actions, not just preparing for them. Trahaearn couldn't force them to follow him, but he hated seeing the change in someone he thought of as a friend.

"It's not the humans. It's Kali. Her influence is growing." Could she have gained so much so soon?

"Whatever it is, we are losing ground. What happens if she manages to start a war while you are closeted with the human leaders?" Quinn stepped forward. "Which way?"

Trahaearn pointed to his left. "I don't know, and I have no control over it. When we find Lionel and Dionne, I hope that the three of you will be able to keep things peaceful." If Quinn was losing hope, there would be no one that he trusted and was capable of protecting the world while he was in that meeting.

He followed Quinn into the small space where Bluth had died, trying to fight the hopelessness that had fallen on him like a heavy blanket.

Quinn was already holding his hand out watching the spinning twigs when Trahaearn joined him. The air was heavy with the energy left behind by the crowd. The trees here did not have spells soaked into their roots to clear the hatred.

He stood silently as the twigs aligned, facing east. If they had any luck left, Lionel and Dionne would be close by and unharmed. It was hard to be hopeful, but perhaps when they were reunited, Quinn's mood would clear.

"Help." The cry was weak and pain threaded through the one word.

Trahaearn turned toward the source, a pile of undergrowth at the edge of the blood-soaked earth.

Quinn put the twigs in his pocket and helped to clear the worst of the dry growth. Trahaearn could smell death.

"Please..." the voice wheezed.

As they lifted the branches, Jeremiah Nielson rolled over on his back. His clothes cut away from his body, the skin on his torso and legs flayed.

"Please make it stop." The words were barely audible.

Trahaearn reached out with a spell to dull the man's pain. He was beyond healing, but at least they could make his death easier.

Nielson stopped struggling to reach them, his face relaxed as the pain stopped. Then his breath rattled and his spirit left his body.

"Kali?" Quinn asked.

"I hope she is the only one capable of causing this," Trahaearn answered.

He placed his hand on the soil beside the body. Reaching out to the spirit of the earth, Trahaearn asked it to take the human's corpse. He'd seen enough graveyards in his travels to know that humans buried their dead. He didn't know what ceremony was needed, but he knew that if the body was found it would be bad.

The spirit of the earth turned the soil to quicksand and Nielson's body sank through it. When it was done, the soil returned to its original state.

"This has gone too far," Quinn said echoing Trahaearn's thoughts.

"We must hurry to find —."

"No," Quinn said. "I will find them. You must focus on solving this. You must find a way to stop Kali."

. . .

GARETH MET TRAHAEARN AT THE DOOR WITH A MUG OF TEA. IT was perfect, as though the man had been gifted with some extra power to know exactly what someone needed. Perhaps that is why he was the grove steward.

Leaving Quinn to the search and returning to the museum was the hardest thing he'd ever done. Finding Lionel and Dionne was something that could be accomplished, and in a short time, and regardless of their condition, they would be found. Nothing about that job was ambiguous or slippery. Everything about dealing with Kali, and sorting out the world, was a chore that seemed like it would never be accomplished.

"Drink the tea," Gareth said. The druid was becoming more normal. He'd lost the hesitancy that weakened his words just after he recovered.

Trahaearn obeyed, swallowing half the mugful when he realized it wasn't hot enough to burn. As he felt the liquid slide down his throat, a sense of peace lifted the hopelessness.

"What was in that?" He couldn't afford to have his senses muddled by a sleeping draught, or any other herbal remedy.

"Nothing you need to worry about," Gareth said. "It's just something to counteract that Kali person. I can feel her every time I step outside the museum."

So, their home was still a sanctuary that Kali couldn't poison. Would it benefit them to hold this meeting of leaders here?

"Where is that phone?" There might be time if he could talk to Jacob now. He patted his pockets and swore when they were empty.

"Here," Gareth held out the device. "It was ringing earlier. I found it on the table."

"Who called?"

"I don't know. By the time I realized what the noise was, it had stopped." Gareth took the empty mug and left Trahaearn alone in the hall.

He opened the phone before realizing that he didn't know

Jacob's number. In fact, he didn't know how to contact any of the humans who could be allies.

The magical folk didn't use technology. If they needed to speak to anyone, they simply drew a circle on the soil and called the person to them. Humans probably wouldn't even hear that type of call.

If Dionne were here, she would know how to deal with this. Trahaearn dropped the phone in his pocket and went looking for Gareth.

In the kitchen, he was surprised to see six of his druids at the table. The sight was a welcome surprise for a change. He greeted the newly healed druids and asked for another mug of the tea.

"It is helping to clear my mind, but I fear I will need more than just one pot." The attempt at humor was unsuccessful. Perhaps they needed a little more time to adjust to the world. They'd been trapped for centuries so it must be disconcerting.

"Someone is coming to the door," Gareth said.

It was good to know that when fully healed, these druids were strong and capable. As steward, Gareth's senses would be able to read the surrounding forest and assess danger, or help. When the world was safe, Trahaearn wouldn't have to rebuild the grove.

"I'll go," Trahaearn said. "It's probably for me, trouble or otherwise." Still not even a chuckle.

By the time Trahaearn reached the top of the stairs, the visitor was knocking on the door. He opened it to see Angela standing there, alone. That was probably not smart given the actions of Kali's followers. Trahaearn couldn't tell if it was bravery on Angela's part, or whether she simply didn't know yet about what happened.

"I have information," Angela said as she entered.

Trahaearn led her to the small room they'd used before, trusting Gareth to know if refreshments were needed. When they were sitting, he prompted, "Do you know how we can deal with Kali?"

"Dealing with a goddess is not a simple thing. What is it you expect to be able to do?"

It was a fair question, and Trahaearn knew he'd have to bring the humans closer to his plans. He just didn't quite feel the trust. Perhaps it was a lingering effect of Kali's power.

"I'll answer your question in a moment, but I need you to understand how we think of these beings." He waited for her to nod. "She calls herself Kali. The last one called herself The Morrigan. Both of these names are in the human mythology. This being is not Kali. Not as you believe her to be. She is not your goddess."

This seemed to surprise Angela. She frowned and thought for a moment before speaking again. "Then why do you need to know about my Kali?"

"Because the being we are dealing with has taken on that goddess's aspects. She will never be your goddess, but she will become more and more like her. By now, the mythology that you believe will have power over her. It comes from the people who follow her. The worshippers of that goddess are weaving a life for this one. They aren't doing it consciously, but it is happening."

Angela shook her head. "I don't think the distinction will matter to the Kali worshippers. If she isn't real — sorry that's how I have to think of it — then how will the legend that surrounds her help?"

The woman would make a good druid, if women could be druids. She had a keen mind and didn't seem to be offended by the discussion of a goddess.

"If the legend contains information on how she can be controlled, or softened, then we can create, or summon that thing or being." He knew it sounded simple, but it would not be in any way easy.

"And your plan?"

"This world, the magical folk and the humans, will not survive if Kali remains the way she is now. There is always a being, a goddess if that's easier, of death and birth. They always seem to have both and that allows a balance. Kali only wants death. We need to turn her from that path. If necessary, and possible, we will banish her. I have no idea how, but I'll have my druids start searching the library." He couldn't leave it there. He had to give her the whole picture. "My hope is that she can be balanced. We do not know who will come after her if we banish Kali. I'm sure she is not the harshest of the goddesses."

Angela stood. "I have only the common knowledge of the legend. If you are right, we need to confirm the truth with the priests. I do not want to send you on a path that is only lit by myths and fairy stories." She laughed. "Although, I suppose the fairy stories are now living with us."

Her laugh lightened Trahaearn's heart.

"How soon will you be able to return?" he asked. If the priests weren't able to help today, the cause may already be lost.

"I will go to the temple now. I cannot promise that what I learn will help you. I cannot even promise that I will return, because if this world is where Kali should be, the priests will not help us to destroy her. If they determine she must live, then I will not be party to your plans." She took a few steps before turning, clearly expecting an escort.

There was nothing Trahaearn could say to Angela's statement. He led her to the door, sent his senses outside to check the mood of the people in the clearing and then, finding no threat, opened the door.

"I will hope for your return," he said.

Angela walked away without responding.

18

Trahaearn watched Angela until she entered the trees. Another thing he needed to wait for before acting; another thing that he couldn't control directly. It wasn't satisfying to let everyone else do the work. Jacob arranging the meetings, Angela gathering intelligence, Quinn handling the other council members — rescuing people that he, Trahaearn Arch Druid, had put in danger.

Despite his efforts, it had been four days of nothing but delay, frustration, and disaster.

He closed the door and called out to his researchers. "Allun, Ceredig, meet me in the archives." If he had to wait, he'd do his own research. There must be something in the archives about handling beings like Kali. Even if there were nothing about banishing, there would be something about how to negotiate their egos. That was one thing these elemental beings had in common: huge egos.

Allun and Ceredig joined him at the table set out specifically for researchers. The table was large enough to hold multiple books and scrolls as well as note taking paper. It was tall enough for the druids to stand as they worked.

He asked what they knew about the world.

"We have been briefed," Allun said.

"It is good to be here among the books," Ceredig said. "What do you need from us?"

"I have someone checking on the human legend of Kali, but I think we need some guidance from the past. If I can negotiate with her, perhaps we can get past this current crisis. It is not in her best interest to kill everyone in the world, as she seems bent on doing."

Allun wandered away and started collecting books.

Ceredig pulled papers from a shelf below the tabletop. "I assume we need to get this done now?" He grinned. "Or perhaps, yesterday would be better."

Trahaearn clapped him on the arm, Ceredig's humor lightening his own mood. "If any druid has found a way to control time, it would be best."

"You need rest, Arch Druid," Ceredig said as he looked to the rows of shelves holding centuries of druidic knowledge. "If you are to meet with these leaders, then you must look less like you are about to fall over."

"There is no time."

"One hour." Ceredig took a step toward the knowledge. His movement was sure, as if something were drawing him to the right book. "Have Markel give you a potion so you rest for an hour. We will have news for you then."

He didn't wait for a response, his steps sped up and Trahaearn was certain that the man was casting a spell to find the information they needed. Researchers had magic that even he didn't understand.

ONE HOUR OF REST UNDER THE HANDS OF THE GROVE HEALER was worth a week's sleep. Trahaearn ran up the stairs to the archives. His optimism had returned along with his health.

Stepping into the room, he saw Allun and Ceredig talking at the table. Their words were too quiet for him to make out what they were saying, but the way each waved his arms and pointed made it clear they were in disagreement.

Good. That meant they had something.

"Well?"

Both men turned to him, but it was Ceredig, the more senior, who spoke. "We have found something that may be useful."

"You were arguing." Trahaearn knew he would get both sides of the argument, but he didn't have the time for a lengthy lecture on the philosophical differences.

"Yes, but not about the information. We have different opinions on the usefulness. I believe you should wait until we have more information on this Kali. Wait until this human brings you her legend."

Allun stepped forward. "I believe you have the skills, Arch Druid, to use the information now."

Good to know that his druids were capable of thinking beyond the task they were given. He'd reserve judgment on Allun's need to suck up to his boss. "What information do you have?"

Ceredig handed him a drawing. It was an intricate circle, one that left only a small space in the center. "It's to summon Kali. You need the extra layers of power to hold her, and it will start to unravel layer by layer once she is inside. You cannot hold her for more than a few minutes, perhaps ten."

Ten minutes to convince Kali to take the long view? Ten minutes to trick her into telling him how to banish her? "Can we cast it more than once?"

"No," Allun said. "There are other designs, but they need rare ingredients that we may not have." He tapped the paper. "This one can only be used once. Perhaps my colleague is correct, and you should not use it before you have all the information you need."

"It would be foolish to waste the effort." Trahaearn couldn't help but feel that he should try, but if he wanted Kali to see the long game, then he couldn't just act on instinct. "Search our supplies for the ingredients we need for the other circles."

"Most of them were in the lab. The vampires destroyed so much of our inventory that I doubt we'll find what we need," Ceredig said. He picked up another paper that had a short list written on it. Shrugging as if to throw off the weight of his words, he continued, "We won't know until we look."

Trahaearn watched the two druids muttering together as they descended the stairs. Could one thing go right? He traced the design of the summoning circle with his finger. Drawing it in salt would take almost as long as it was expected to last. Ceredig was wise, they needed to keep this until they had a plan.

IF SHE HAD MORE POWER, KALI KNEW THAT SHE'D BE ABLE TO watch everyone and everything. Until she won this battle with the druid, she would have to settle for seeking out those she needed to control.

The druid had avoided her trap but only by chance. Hiding that fool Nielson's body was unexpected. Kali had hoped the humans would think the druid was killing anyone who entered his domain. She would have to be less subtle. She needed a new dupe. Glen was too useful to kill, yet.

She hovered behind the veil seeking opportunities. The world beyond was harder to see, the veil was thicker, more like a curtain. Was this a warning of something? Was she taking too long to control her opposition? She reached out and this time, instead of a cool whisper against her skin, she felt substance, not silk or lace, but a thick, heavy weave that resisted her efforts. She was still able to penetrate this new version, and still able to spy through it, if with difficulty. If the veil continued to coalesce, that might change.

Fear flooded her. This was a new emotion. One that drained her energy. The druid was changing the veil. He had found a way to stop her. She slipped through before it could trap her in the other world.

It was an alley.

There were no other beings in sight. A warm scent of hatred and imminent violence drew her toward the edge of the shadows. There was energy here for her to take, not enough to sustain her, but enough that she could edge it into killing with no effort.

Killing was not the only objective. Kali needed a killing that would point to the druids. A killing that would cause Trahaearn to lose his standing in the human world. With that accomplished, there would be no one to negotiate peace.

Three men marched a fourth into the alley, and then pushed him up against a wall. The victim was older than the attackers. His fear soaked into her being, but did not show on his face, or in his voice.

"You don't want to do this," he said calmly.

"Magic lover," the one who held him against the wall accused. "We need to destroy these creatures before they destroy us."

Kali smelled the sour odor of stale alcohol on the attacker's breath. It added a veneer of strength to the hate that she drew from him.

Kali rode the fear and entered the victim's mind. "You must fight, or they will slaughter you."

Her suggestion twisted his fear into something closer to rage.

"If you don't let me go, I will have no choice but to..." his words petered out. The man didn't know what to say.

"To what? To fight?" Another of the attackers lunged in, stopping with his face only inches from the victim. This man's clothes were stained with grease so deeply that Kali wondered if they had ever been clean. "You? Come on then."

Kali noticed a wink of yellow light as it caught the attention of the third thug. "What the... One of them is down there."

"Not a chance," the first thug said. "It's just the sun. The freaks are hiding out."

Kali slid her thoughts into the first thug's mind and planted an image of a druid. She wasn't strong enough to make it look like Trahaearn, but she was able to easily plant the idea that it was him through the drunken haze of his thoughts.

"Shit," he said. "That one is out of his cage."

The other two thugs looked around.

While their attention was focused on the appearance of magic, the victim struggled for freedom.

Kali had lost control of the man's mind. She returned to him. If her plan was to work, this man, this unlikely man, must be the witness. He would be the one to lay the murders at Trahaearn's feet.

It was draining for her to manage two minds, but she could renew her energy from the murders. Keeping the victim unable to see what was actually happening by ensuring the three thugs remained crowded around him, she inserted a memory of being attacked in the mind of the thug in soiled clothes.

"What the fuck," he screamed. He clutched his arm as if it had been sliced open and he was containing the blood.

As the middle thug, a pale thin wraith of a man, turned away from staring at the mirage she'd created, he doubled over, sure that he'd been stabbed in the gut.

She was enjoying the emotions that were flowing from the humans. Forcing the victim to close his eyes, she caused the wraith to believe he had been attacked by his companion.

That was all it took.

Kali sent a mist of her essence into the human who would survive and reinforced his assumptions about what he could hear. While she worked, Kali kept the man terrified to ensure he would not open his eyes.

The three thugs drew knives on each other. Her witness sank

to the ground as soon as he was released, then rolled into a ball, arms over his head.

As Kali watched, the thugs sliced at each other, the image of the druid she'd created forgotten in their burning need to kill before they were killed.

Flesh parted as a blade slashed. In no time the thin one lay on the hard surface of the alley, his gut split open, his life flowing out of him with the blood. Kali fought the urge to laugh in joy at the power she was absorbing.

His breath rattled, and then he was dead.

The drunken thug dodged his fellow's knife and stuck his own blade into the man's neck. Then he stood back to watch his former companion die.

Kali needed them all dead.

She needed this one last life to be taken.

Her witness was too far gone in his fear to do it and he needed to be innocent of this violence. She feared that his terror would stop him from telling his version. It would be better for this story to be told immediately, but even if it took an entire day, Trahaearn would wear this crime.

The dying man was her only real choice. She looked at him, his clothes even dirtier from the grime on the ground and the pool of blood. He should be welcoming the relief of death if life had brought him this low. She struggled with the last reserves of her energy and gave him enough to lunge at his attacker. It was clumsy, but she ensured that his knife sank into the gut of the drunken thug as they fell to the ground, entangled in their deaths.

❧ 19 ❧

There was nothing for Trahaearn to do but wait. For Jacob to arrange the meeting, for Quinn to find Dionne and Lionel, and for Angela to return from her priests.

It felt cowardly to stay inside the museum, but Trahaearn couldn't help but feel that it was the wisest move. If he was inside, then he couldn't be dragged into something foolish, or dangerous.

Rest, food, and a visit with his druids would fill the time until he could act again. He returned to the kitchen, no other druids had woken, and his two researchers were still deep in the archives.

"Do we expect everyone to recover," he asked Markel, taking a bowl of stew and a heel of the fresh bread to the table. It had been too long since he'd had more than a stopgap snack.

"It will be a few days," Markel answered. He was grinding herbs in a bowl. "I am doing as much as I can to heal them enough for their own spirits to take over. We may lose two of our number but that is not certain."

Trahaearn nodded. "Let's hope that we are all enjoying a meal together in a few days. If the world is not put to right by then, we are all lost anyway."

Markel nodded and continued grinding. "No matter how bad today seems, it is better than being in the amulet."

Trahaearn remembered the few minutes he'd spent in there before releasing the druid spirits; the empty unending corridors of light, the feeling that something was about to attack, the screams of the trapped souls. "I wouldn't wish even Kali to spend time there." Perhaps she would find sustenance there, but he had spoken the truth to Markel.

"Do you know why your bodies didn't age in there?" It had been a boon when they were trying to rescue the druids, but now, with time to think, it seemed an odd boon.

Markel added a few more sprigs of something to the bowl and pressed the pestle into the mash. "It is something we will be discussing for as long as we draw breath, I think. My opinion is that the vampire spirits acted on our bodies as if they were vampire bodies. You remember they were immortal. Prone to being killed, but never dying."

"I don't suppose anyone will volunteer as a test subject for any of the hypotheses," Trahaearn said, grinning.

Gareth entered the room. "There is a summoning spell in the workroom. I believe the park guardian is calling you."

Beacon? That couldn't be good.

Trahaearn thanked the two druids and slipped out of the room to descend the stairs so that he could draw a circle in the earth and answer the sprite's call.

Beacon didn't spend time on pleasantries. "There's bad news."

"Is there any other kind?" Trahaearn motioned for Beacon to continue.

"Folk are coming from other areas to join us in the park. One of them, a brownie, passed through the city today. He thought it was safer to travel in the light. It hides most of his glow."

"It's probably best. Are you having problems protecting everyone? Do you need to send some of your charges to the museum?" They could take a large number of fairies, or pixies, or even the smaller sprites. But that would complicate things when the humans came.

"No, we are fine. This brownie saw Kali. He says she caused three humans to die and that she made it seem like your fault."

So much for staying inside the museum and out of trouble. "How did she make me the culprit?"

"Another human, no wait. Let him tell you."

Beacon's image held out his hand and a brownie hopped onto the palm. Less than a foot tall, he was dressed in brown rags. A belt around his hips held a variety of tools.

The brownie bowed to Trahaearn. "Salutations. My name is Greensaw, and I am in your debt for creating this haven."

Trahaearn knew that the brownie wouldn't give his information until the proper greetings were exchanged. If he tried to skip to the meat of the conversation, the brownie would keep starting it, because they were creatures of protocol first and gossip second. "We are honored by your presence, Greensaw. Let us both wish for the haven to become permanent."

"If that is to happen, you need to stop this blue woman from painting you a murderer. I was at the edge of the shadows. The humans saw me but convinced themselves that I was not there. I am quite lucky."

Trahaearn waited for Greensaw to continue.

"I watched her make them fight. Three humans. All dead. There was one more who wisely kept himself out of the way. She made them say things like 'the druid was there'. The wise one only heard what happened. He did not see them attack. He will tell the other humans that you did this thing."

Kali was getting smarter while he was stuck waiting for information. Trahaearn asked for details on where the fight happened. He would have to do something to stop the man from talking. If he could cast a spell that erased his memory of the fight, it would help, but that was risky. The spell might take too much of the man's mind.

Beacon thanked Greensaw and placed him on the ground and out of the spell. "It's only one alley away from Banks," he said.

"Do you think Maeve can take him in? Do something to heal the man's mind." Trahaearn knew that the sidhe had subtler spells. Their constant maneuvering for Maeve's favor might have produced a useful charm.

"If not, she can hold him in thrall until this is over." Beacon slumped. "It feels like we are sinking further into the mess. Is there going to be a solution?"

Trahaearn hated the despondency he saw in Beacon. If it continued, the park would begin to fade and that would put all of the people who had fled there for sanctuary in danger. Not to mention the damage to the ancient trees. "Perhaps we have reached the darkest moment in this struggle." That didn't sound encouraging. Beacon needed hope not harsh truth. "There are signs that we will survive this. The human leaders are willing to meet with me. If we can get them to believe we are not a threat, in fact that we might be of benefit, we will be fine. As the leaders act, eventually the rest of the humans will follow."

Beacon didn't seem to take comfort from his words. "I'll get Maeve to deal with the human. I will let you know if there is any other problem."

Trahaearn thanked Beacon and they both broke the circle.

Maeve would extract a price for this. Even though all of the Real… no magical folk would survive or die based on what Trahaearn could arrange with the humans, Maeve would see this as a favor she was doing for the druids. That was something to deal with later. And dealing with magical folk was something more familiar.

Trahaearn cast his senses into the soil. If they were going to have to summon Kali, he wanted the spell to be pure, no lingering trace of previous circles to weaken the summoning. Minutes later, satisfied there would be no problem, he left the room.

As he approached the doorway to the kitchen, he caught the

sound of Jacob's voice. Hope lightened his steps. If the man had returned, they must be ready for the meeting.

He stopped just inside the archway. Jacob was sitting at the table next to Lionel and Dionne.

"Where is Quinn?" Trahaearn asked as he joined them. "Where were you?"

"Someone must have thrown a disorientation charm at us," Dionne said. Her eyes flicked to Lionel in conspiracy or accusation.

Trahaearn was sure it would make a good story whatever the look meant. Now they didn't have time for stories. "So, you have simply been lost?"

"Yes," Lionel said, a slight cough betraying his discomfort. "We seem to have been in the woods around the museum this entire time. Well, I say entire time, but it has only been an hour, perhaps a little longer."

Dionne picked up the conversation, leaving no time for questions. "We bumped into Jacob. I guess that broke the spell. We came back here since that's where he was going." She frowned and then asked, "What do you mean where's Quinn? Is he lost?"

Trahaearn sincerely hoped not. "He's looking for you."

Lionel stood, poking Dionne so she would join him. "We should probably find him."

As much as he wanted to avoid losing them again, Trahaearn knew that Quinn needed these two to be safe. They had both come close to dying, or worse, in the effort to bring the prophecy to fruition, and to save the druids. "He was following your twig spell. I suppose you could wait here for him, but it might take a while for the trail to bring him back."

Dionne tugged at Lionel. "We'll backtrack. It should speed things up," she said. "As soon as we find him, we'll come back. You need us."

Trahaearn wouldn't put them in danger again. Even if Quinn let them return, the museum was not going to be a sanctuary for much longer. The reality was that Kali would probably be drawn to the building soon and that would endanger anyone within its walls.

He needed to give them a task, something that would fill their desire to help. Preferably something that would actually help.

"I need ambassadors to the others." He explained what Beacon was doing for him. "If you can ensure that Maeve takes care of the human, it will help. Dionne, please remember the humans know you are a witch. If it is not too high a risk, please keep the sidhe and the forest folk from acting alone. I need only..." he looked at Jacob. "How long will it be until we meet with the leaders?"

"Tonight," he said. "It might take a couple of days to get agreement, but if you are successful, most of the humans will follow it — eventually."

One more obstacle and they would be done, for good or bad. "It seems I only need them to cooperate for a few days. Why does that feel like centuries?"

Lionel dug into his pocket. "We'll do our best, but you won't be able to get to a circle while you are with the humans. Here's a charm that we can use to communicate."

Trahaearn accepted the ball of leaves.

"Oh my god!" Dionne exclaimed. "You need to get a phone."

Jacob laughed. "He has one, but I think it will take more than a couple of days for them to break the habit." He gave Dionne the number. "Call the phone and he'll be able to use that. I despair of teaching him to use contacts, or texting."

Dionne laughed and pressed the numbers then ended the call.

Trahaearn heard the phone ring then cut off. He would have to rely on Jacob to explain what he was supposed to do.

"Go and be safe," he said as Dionne and Lionel ran for the door.

Trahaearn checked the state of the clearing outside the museum. He wasn't going to let Jacob walk out into an ambush. The fact that the mob had left was no guarantee that they wouldn't come back. It had only been a few hours, so nothing was sure.

"I'll be back in time to escort you," Jacob said. Then, glancing at Trahaearn's clothes, he added, "If you could look more... ceremonial it might help."

Trahaearn didn't need to look at his robes to know they were covered in dirt from the tunnel, and his time in the earth, and the general mess of running around reacting to everything that was being thrown at him. Druids didn't react to others; they led the way. "I'll dress in something that is appropriate for the sidhe court: formal, but not ornate. How will that be?" As much as he wanted to ignore his clothing for other more pressing problems, he knew that the impression he gave would affect how the humans saw the magical folk.

"Yeah, that's probably okay." Jacob turned to start across the threshold when he stopped. "I forgot to mention something." He paused and looked at Trahaearn again, this time frowning. "There might — no strike that, there definitely will be some security people coming to you. You need to answer their questions, so they don't call off the summit for the safety of the leaders."

"And will they know what kind of threat I might present? Are they conversant in spells?" He tried to add a little humor to his tone, but his irritation shone through.

"Yeah. Don't take that attitude with them. They won't be asking about spells, but they will be checking your attitude." He turned away again. "You have another visitor."

Past Jacob's shoulder Trahaearn could see Angela striding across the grass toward him. This time she had a pair of bodyguards trailing her. Jacob passed Angela as he left, nodding at the guards before continuing.

Trahaearn held the door wide. "I hope you feel safe with me, Angela."

She looked at the two men in dark suits and sunglasses. "They are not with me. Or rather, they are, but it's because I'll be at the summit and they are following me to ensure I'm not some kind of crazed terrorist." She rolled her eyes. "I believe they want to question you as well."

Wishing Jacob had warned him earlier, Trahaearn made the security team welcome in the hall. "I hope you can wait until Angela and I have concluded our business." He made it a statement rather than a question.

"We'll wait here," the taller one said.

"I am Trahaearn, Arch Druid." He waited until one of them offered a name.

"Agent Green. This is Agent Wilson. We represent the security forces for the summit." Green volunteered nothing else. They stared with an intensity that unsettled Trahaearn. Even from behind the sunglasses, he could feel the power of their suppressed menace. They looked like two different versions of the same person. Agent Green a few inches taller, agent Wilson a little more muscular. It was a good tactic, he thought, the similarity seemed to take away their humanity and replace it with something impersonal and capable.

Trahaearn ushered Angela into the small room, glad neither agent insisted on following. If they heard about the danger Kali posed, there was no doubt in his mind that the summit would be cancelled.

"Have you found anything we can use?" he asked.

"I have confirmation of the legend. It's surprisingly close to the common understanding. There is a way to calm her, but I don't know if... No, I forget that I don't have a clue what you can or can't do. Let me tell you the legend, and then we can talk about what you might be able to do about it."

Trahaearn gestured for Angela to continue. She knew the urgency of this; he trusted that she wouldn't dally in the telling.

"Kali is not only the goddess of death and birth; she is also charged with time and change. I suppose that is why she came now. Anyway, this being who calls herself Kali is enough like the legend that perhaps the solution is transferable."

Trahaearn bit back a command to hurry. "I think since she has taken on the name and image, she will be bound by the constraints of what her human worshippers believe."

"Good. The legend states that in coming to the aid of another who is trying to slay a demon, Kali realizes that every drop of blood that falls produces a duplicate of the demon. She draws on her power and slays the demon by drinking every last drop of blood from his body and devouring his duplicates as they form. Her victory dance upon the fallen is said to have consumed her, making her unable and unwilling to stop herself from stamping the fallen into the ground. Kali is the consort of God Shiva. To break the control of her bloodlust, he lay down amongst the dead beneath her feet. The instant her foot touched her beloved Shiva she was able see more than just death."

Trahaearn felt real hope for the first time in days. "She represents chaos that comes with change?"

"Yes, initially," Angela said. "Is there a way for you to summon God Shiva?" There was fear and awe in her voice.

It must be hard to remember that their gods were different from the ones that seem to rule the world. "We should be able to summon what Kali will see as this Shiva. It will not be your god, any more than Kali is your goddess. But the symbol will be sufficient. And it is time that the world came out of chaos, I think."

Relief radiated from Angela. "What can I do to help?"

Trahaearn could sympathize. Who would not want to meet their god? "I will get my researchers to find the summoning that will bring Shiva and Kali together. Perhaps you can tell me how to assure the men waiting outside that I am not a threat."

"They will always think that you are a threat," Angela said, chuckling. "They just need to know they can handle you. I don't know how to help with that."

Trahaearn walked Angela to the door and watched as she left the clearing. She made him feel comfortable and that was what he hoped for all the humans. It would be something to work on once they were past this first hurdle.

He returned to the two agents.

"You have questions?" Trahaearn ushered them toward the kitchen. "I need to eat, so if you don't mind, we can do this downstairs."

Agent Green nodded and touched his ear, muttering something to an invisible listener. As he passed Trahaearn, the druid noticed a clear cable running from behind his ear and under the collar of his jacket.

Some sort of phone.

They descended the stairs. Agent Green in front and agent Wilson at the rear. Trahaearn between them wondering what they felt they needed to protect him from in his own home.

When they were seated around the table, Trahaearn asked, "What do you need to know?" He wasn't going to offer information.

Gareth placed a bowl of stew in front of Trahaearn and two mugs of tea in front of the agents before leaving them alone. The men glanced down but neither took a sip.

Agent Green looked around before saying, "We need to ensure that you are not going to be a danger to the people in the meeting. Our usual methods won't work. None of you have any history in our systems."

Trahaearn nodded. There was nothing he could say to that statement.

Agent Wilson shifted his shoulders as if he needed to spring into action. "Your representative, Jacob Myers, he says you can take an oath. I guess it's not the same as swearing on the Bible, or whatever."

So, Jacob had promoted himself to their representative. It was probably a fair assessment of his role. Trahaearn knew what the Bible meant to humans, but he didn't know how effective swearing on it would be. "What happens to someone who swears on your Bible and then breaks the oath?"

"Maybe they go to prison, maybe they don't," agent Green said. "It's not my job to check."

"When we take an oath, there are always consequences. There is no maybe about it. If I were to take an oath that required me to keep the humans in this room safe, and I didn't act on a threat, I would suffer the penalty which is declared in the oath."

Agent Wilson glanced at his partner and must have received some indication of what to do, because he asked, "How would we know that is true?"

Trahaearn would have asked the same question if the situation were reversed. "I will have someone write out the actual oath which you can read before agreeing. For my benefit, there must be some limitation built in. Nothing to concern you, but I cannot take a lifetime oath." *Not for my lifetime anyway.* "If you would permit, I can demonstrate on one of you."

Agent Wilson paled, but to his credit nodded. "What would that entail?"

Trahaearn pushed aside the half-eaten stew. "One of you would take an oath, limited to one action. The consequences would be minor, and then we test the oath."

The two agents exchanged glances again. This time agent Green spoke. "I don't like it, but if it works, we can sign off on your attendance."

Since the summit was all about the way humans and magical folk inhabited the same world, it would be useless without him. Trahaearn kept the thought to himself. "The oath I will take at that time will have more serious repercussions, but perhaps this will work as a test. I will have one of you take an oath not to speak the words *rabbit stew*, and if you do, you will leave the room. Then you will say rabbit stew and we'll see if you can stop yourself from leaving."

"I'll do it," Agent Wilson said. "How long will it last?"

Trahaearn knew by the way his shoulders tensed how hard it was for this man to give over control to anyone else. "Only the one time."

"Let's do it. Do you need my blood or anything?"

"Not for something this minor. Give me a moment." Trahaearn went to the cupboard and took out two bay leaves. Returning to the table, he said, "We will say the words, and the oath will take effect when we crush these leaves between our hands."

He placed the leaves in agent Wilson's palm. "Repeat these words. I will not utter the words rabbit stew within the next five minutes. If I break my oath, I will leave the room and wait until I am invited back."

Agent Wilson repeated the oath. Trahaearn clasped his hand and they squeezed until the leaves crumbled.

Before Agent Wilson could test the oath, Trahaearn asked, "Do you feel anything different?"

"Nothing. Did it work?"

Trahaearn looked at Agent Green. "Does he look or sound different?"

"No."

It would have helped if humans felt the weight of the oath, but perhaps it was too light a burden for them to feel. Trahaearn motioned for Agent Wilson to violate the oath.

The man stuttered a few times before saying the two words. As soon as the final syllable left his mouth, Agent Wilson stood and marched to the door, waiting just outside.

"Please, come back," Trahaearn said.

"I felt something holding me back from even saying it, so I guess it worked."

"Try again," Trahaearn said, wanting to assure the man that the oath was gone.

"Rabbit stew. Yeah, it's different." Agent Wilson nodded to his partner. "This will work, but we need to brief everyone."

The two men rose, Agent Green taking the lead. "We'll be in touch, and we'll have a list of things we need covered by the oath."

Trahaearn picked up his stew and followed the agents to the door.

21

Too long.

Kali could feel the veil thicken. She needed more energy to push through to the human world. She was losing the battle with the druid. The death count wasn't high enough to power her for long. She needed to destroy him in the minds of the humans. Somehow the news of the three dead men hadn't yet gotten out.

It was time to make her new cult leader act. She would not pass the veil this time. There was too much chance that she would be trapped on the other side.

She could sense Glen near the museum. His mind was torn. The man wanted power so much that he was afraid to make the wrong decision. She could almost read the thoughts in his energy. He would be on the winning side no matter what. If he acted for Kali and she lost, he would claim he was the instrument of her downfall. If she won, he would be by her side. It amused her that he didn't consider the cost of being by her side.

"Glen," she whispered into his mind. She saw him twitch in surprise, but the veil clouded the details of his expression. Only a few hours ago, the veil had been as clear as a pane of glass.

"Where are you?" He moved to put a tree between him and the clearing to the museum before looking around.

"I will not show myself again until I am victorious."

"Do you have a message for me?"

Kali smiled and sipped energy from his ambition. He so desperately wanted to be seen as the hero, and standing watch was far from heroic. If this type of energy could sustain her, she would be powerful already. This world was full of humans and magical creatures who wanted to be more important, richer, or more influential. But it was not enough. The energy of ambition faded almost as soon as she took it in.

"The druid murdered some of my followers. The world must know him as the killer he really is. They must fear him."

She watched his mind sift through the options. If he accused the druid of this crime, there was little chance he could change his allegiance if things went against Kali. She nudged his thoughts toward her side. It was obvious that the druid and his kind were weak. Kali would be victorious.

It took little of her precious power to push him to her side.

"I can tell the world. Where are these bodies?"

He was hers.

Kali would use him and then drink his spirit when she sacrificed him.

"In an alley in the city." She placed an image in his mind of the three bodies. "There was a witness, but he is gone."

Glen moved away from the tree and started walking toward the location. Kali knew he would not deviate from the task. He was compelled to the site of the bodies. She watched him take out a device and tap the glass.

"I have a hot story for you," he said, holding the device to his ear. "You'll want this as an exclusive. Yes, I'm telling you this will shine a new light on the situation."

After listening for a moment, he gave the location of the bodies.

Kali drifted away, seeking bloodshed to fuel her.

THE PHONE RANG. TRAHAEARN PUSHED ASIDE THE PAPERS HE'D been researching. No hints on summoning a being called Shiva, yet. He grabbed the device and flipped it open.

"Trahaearn?" Jacob's voice came through.

"Yes." It was hard to communicate without even an image of a person.

"Usually we say hello when we answer," Jacob said. "I have bad news."

"That's all we seem to get these days. What is it?"

"Three bodies were found on the east side of town. Glen is telling the world that you killed them. He says he has proof, but no one has seen it yet."

Beacon hadn't been fast enough.

"Why is Glen doing this?" Trahaearn hadn't suspected that they would be betrayed from within. The two humans seemed genuinely on the magical folks' side.

"Maybe Kali got to him?" Jacob sounded unsure.

"Did he mention her?" If Kali was in the open, then they only had one priority, find Shiva, and get her calmed down.

"No, at least not yet. He's planning a press conference, and he's getting attention. If she puts in an appearance, it would be a good time."

Trahaearn was worried that Jacob was so calm. Did the man trust that a druid could deal with anything? "Can you stop him?"

A sigh floated out of the phone. "No. I was hoping you could be available to answer his accusations. The main problem is that the public will start to believe whoever talks the most. They see silence as some kind of admission of guilt."

"How long until I meet with these leaders?" Trahaearn wanted to stay in the museum. This was where his books and scrolls were.

This was where they would find a permanent solution to Kali's bloodthirst.

"A few hours."

If he couldn't get Kali under control before the meeting, she would have free reign until he was done. That could be days. The war could be lost before the humans realized there was a fight. She could set off a reaction that killed everyone in the time he was distracted. "I cannot come out and deal with her. Jacob, I have to find the being that represents Shiva. I know that Kali wouldn't exist without her mate being there. I have to stay. If we find the solution, I have to be here to enact it."

"We need more of you magical folk out in the world. Is there someone who can prove you are not plotting to kill everyone?"

And that was the real problem. It wasn't a case of *if* the humans equated Kali with magical folk; it was simply a question of *when*. Once she'd tarred them with her actions, no agreement would stem the hatred that humans would turn on anything not human.

"Trahaearn?"

"Sorry. I was thinking." He wondered if Maeve would step forward as spokesperson. Could he put their fates in her selfish hands? Quinn, or Dionne, or even Lionel, were better choices. "Maybe you can talk to Dionne. It's just a delay we need. Something to keep people from making up their minds." He gave Quinn's address and ended the call.

He didn't need Jacob to report back. He needed his researchers to find the summoning spell.

It wasn't quite blood lust, but Kali was energized with the confusion and fear building from Glen's announcement.

The humans were so easy to influence. They were constantly floating on the edge of fear and hatred. The flimsiest of stories pulled them to her side. It would only take a few more tales, a few more deaths.

The druid didn't even bother to come out of his museum. She would use that. If he wasn't going to fight back, it would take less energy to start the fire that would feed her for eternity.

The veil was back to its flimsy transparent state. Her energy must be high enough to transfer between the worlds again. It was time to claim victory over the druid. She would enjoy his reaction.

Slipping through the veil into the museum where she sensed Trahaearn, Kali found herself in a dimly lit room. Books and scrolls filled the numerous shelves and she could feel the weight of knowledge residing in them. It wouldn't matter how much information the druids had collected, there would soon be no one to read the words that contained the wisdom.

"Are you afraid of me?" she asked.

Trahaearn turned at the sound of her voice, his usual poise lost as he realized she'd come to him. He recovered quickly or seemed to anyway. Kali still had difficulty reading the man's thoughts.

"No more than common sense suggests I should be. You are a danger to this world." He turned over the page he'd been writing on and looked at her directly.

Was the man trying to provoke her?

"You have been denounced," she said. His behavior was simply a cover for his fear, she was certain of that. No one, simple man or druid, could deny her power.

"Yes. You took someone I trusted and made them act against me. Did you enjoy what was said?"

There was that flash of anger. He wasn't as unaffected as he pretended. Kali smiled.

"Yes, I heard your man tell the world that you had killed three humans. There was no one there to deny it." A shiver went through her body.

"Unfortunate, but perhaps I have not yet lost the battle. What else was said?"

The man was determined to show he wasn't afraid of her. Kali held out her hand and allowed the memory of the event to play out on her palm.

Trahaearn watched closely, tilting his head to catch the words. Kali closed her hand at the end, realizing how foolish she'd been for expending energy in that way. No matter. The energy would be replaced soon.

"Did Glen really say that you were one of us?" Trahaearn asked.

Kali smiled. That had been a bonus. Glen was wise to keep her status as a goddess secret. "He said that I was a choice. That I could defeat you, and that I was in possession of more magic than any other being. All of it is true."

"We'll see if it is really true in time," he responded. "What I heard is that he made you a greater danger than I am. The humans will be thinking about that when they get over the shock. They'll ask themselves, if you are so powerful, why didn't you stop the killing? Despite what you think, humans want to live. They will not thank you for drowning the world in blood."

That interpretation had passed her by.

Kali felt anger burning away at her reserve of energy. She was going to be too weak soon to pass through the veil. She chose not to believe the druid's version. "I will leave you now, druid. But think on this. A death is a death. I feed whether the humans love me or not."

She slipped back through the veil, it resisted, but she made it to the other side. Her view of Trahaearn was not reassuring. He simply returned to the paper he'd hidden. She couldn't see the details, just a pretty circle of lines that looked like intricate lace. It tugged at her to come closer, but the veil was too dense.

22

Trahaearn stared at the circle pattern that he'd been practicing. He recalled that Ceredig's best guess was that it would contain Kali for at least ten minutes. The guess was based on less information than anyone would have used before the crisis. He was certain that Kali's appearance as The Morrigan's replacement had done something to strip the world of information about her. It was surprising that the priests had kept their knowledge, but perhaps whatever caused the information to leak from the internet and the libraries, took longer when it was reinforced with belief.

"We have it," Allun's voice broke through Trahaearn's thoughts.

The druid was standing with Ceredig, both grinning victoriously. Allun held a sheet of paper out. There were words scratched in patterns across the page.

Hope bloomed in Trahaearn's chest. "The summoning for Shiva?"

They would win this battle.

"Not quite," Ceredig said.

The warmth of hope fled. "If this is not going to help us rid the world of Kali's bloodlust, why are you smiling?" Did the madness of the amulet infect them still?

"We learned that you cannot summon a being with that much power. Everything is shrouded in secrets and references that lead nowhere."

"Then how did we find this?" Trahaearn asked holding out the circle he'd been studying.

"Ah," Allun said. "If you will listen, Arch Druid, perhaps we can explain the process we followed."

Trahaearn didn't want to listen to a lengthy treatise on research methodology. He didn't have time, and it wouldn't matter if they couldn't act soon. "Just the high points. I promise to listen to every detail if we survive what is coming."

Ceredig looked at his colleague and nodded. "First the circle. When we said it would summon her, we weren't being precise. It will entice her. She will be drawn to it, and will stay as long as its beauty captures her. That's why we think it will only last a short time. Perhaps when you have her, you can distract her long enough to keep it interesting to her."

That's what he got for not listening to the whole story.

Trahaearn knew that important details might be lost if the druids cut too much out of their explanation. "By high points, I mean that kind of detail." Seeing the reaction on their faces, Trahaearn added, "I am more than happy that you found these spells. You have been able to sift through much of the knowledge in only a few hours. You have done well. Now, the information on Shiva."

Ceredig lost his expression of defeat and brightened. He looked at his spell paper as he continued, "This Shiva you will create, is not the same as the God Shiva that the woman spoke about. What we realized is that Kali does not know about the legend, but she will be impacted by it. There was a wonderful history on the relationship between the belief system and the aspect of gods and goddesses." He looked up from the paper.

"Well that may be too much detail. Suffice it to say the proof was there and gave us this plan. We will create, or rather you will create, the Shiva you need. He will only exist as a bundle of the facts that relate to Kali. He will feel real to her and that is all we need."

It was a good plan. "Thank you. This may, indeed, save the world. Explain the process to me. We will cast the circle as soon as we can."

Allun took over the explanation and within a few minutes, Trahaearn had all he needed. The spell would take few ingredients, but it would require power.

"Get everything ready in the work room. I will restore myself and join you."

Trahaearn wanted new power. The only way to do that was leave the museum and sit on clear soil. The workroom power was useful for most purposes, but it was filtered through the walls of spells that protected the druids.

He nodded to the small group of people still seated around their camp, and then walked through the tree line and settled on the ground. Removing his shoes, he placed his soles against the cool moist soil and felt the power of the earth fill him. His tattoos pulsed and then darkened as he became stronger.

The phone rang.

He didn't need to meditate to take on power, but it would have been nice to take a moment of peace. Trahaearn took the phone out and answered it.

Jacob didn't even say hello. "It's getting bad out here, Trahaearn."

An understatement.

"What happened?"

"People are starting to gather. The bigger the crowd the nastier it gets. We'll have a riot on our hands if we can't stop it. I tried to get Dionne to talk to them, but she didn't answer her phone."

Trahaearn didn't think things would simply settle down if Kali stopped pushing. "What do I need to do?" Other than find twice the time in a day than he had.

"You need to speak. Can you come to us?"

"I can't be away for long. Can you meet me? Perhaps at the eastern edge of the woods?" If all they needed was for him to speak, then he would.

"Ten minutes. I'll have cameras. What are you going to say?" Jacob sounded frightened. His confidence washed away in the face of so many setbacks.

"I've got ten minutes to think of something." Trahaearn closed the phone and pulled on his shoes. Thankful that he'd thrown robes over his jeans and teeshirt, he marched to the edge of the trees.

The eastern edge of the forest only covered two blocks. Jacob and three other people arrived in a van only minutes after Trahaearn. In moments, a woman dressed in a suit stood beside Trahaearn, the two men, one with a camera and the other with a microphone, arranged themselves to the side. Jacob had his own camera pointed at them.

There was no time to prepare. The woman started talking. "I'm Donna Travers and this is the Arch Druid Trahaearn. We're here to get the Arch Druid's response to the accusations. Did you kill those men?"

Trahaearn hadn't been able to find the words he needed before, but the woman's statement seemed to evoke his response. "I did not. I cannot believe that there is proof that any of the magical folk committed any crimes."

"But Glen Watson is a respected member of the community. Is there a reason he would lie?"

She was smiling the entire time she attacked him.

"I do not know Mr. Watson's motives. I considered him a colleague, even a friend. I assure you that he is mistaken, or perhaps he is being used to smear the magical folk."

"Will you agree to meet with him? We can arrange for you both to be interviewed."

There was nothing that Trahaearn could say to change what Kali must have done to Glen. The only way to save the man was to calm her bloodlust. Trahaearn realized he had a card to play in this game. "I would be happy to meet with him. It will have to be after I've met with your leaders. The outcomes of that meeting will have global impact. I think that takes precedence over a local misunderstanding."

Jacob didn't look happy with the statement, but he didn't speak.

Donna Travers also seemed to be taken aback. She controlled her expression with a new smile. "I'm sure that Mr. Watson will be agreeable." She turned to the camera. "I'm Donna Travers and that's the situation here in Vancouver."

The cameraman lowered his camera and gave her a thumbs up, the man holding the microphone collapsed the extended handle and walked toward the van.

"Good luck with the summit." Donna didn't sound like she meant it. Probably better news if it failed.

23

"Hey, why do you look like your dog died?" Jacob asked.

Trahaearn turned to him. When had he lost the ability to hide his feelings? Was that a side effect of the prophecy, or perhaps it was the lack of sleep. "It didn't work. She didn't believe me."

"Don't worry, by the time she gets that on the air it will be all over. Look." He held his tablet out for Trahaearn to see. The interview played across the screen.

"So, you made a copy, what does that have to do with anything?"

"I uploaded it a few minutes ago, and it's already hit ten million views." Jacob looked at him as though that should mean something. He sighed and took the tablet back, swiping the screen and then handing it to Trahaearn.

This time he pointed to the lower corner of the screen. "Donna will be pissed off, but she should have known better than to let me stand there with my camera. See that number?"

Trahaearn looked where Jacob pointed. A number was rapidly counting up on the screen. "Twelve million people have seen this?"

"Not only that but look at the map."

Trahaearn looked at the depiction of the world on the screen. It was mostly dark blue with a few patches of light blue. "Is this representative of the audience?"

"Yeah, the whole world is watching. We might break the internet." He slapped Trahaearn on the shoulder. "That's a good thing right now. Look, I can do the analysis, but I'm guessing that the world is willing to give you a chance. That's what we wanted, right?"

Hope lightened the weight on Trahaearn's soul. "Yes. How long? I have something important to do before the summit."

"The summit should be the most important thing on your mind, Trahaearn. Is there something I should know?"

Trahaearn took the time to choose his words carefully. "No agreement will work if Kali is still coercing violence. We need to get her calmed down before I am in the summit. If she has free reign while I meet with these leaders, the world will be covered in blood by the time we finish." The words felt like a mantra, he'd thought them so often.

Jacob stuffed his tablet into his backpack. "I thought you wanted to get rid of her."

"It will be better if we can get her... balanced, is the best word. How long before we need to leave?"

"We have an expression. Better the devil you know. I guess that fits perfectly here. You have an hour. The security guys will come for you. They told me you were going to take an oath. That will have to happen before you leave."

It wouldn't take that much time if everything went to plan. Trahaearn feared that if something went wrong, there would be no time in the world to fix it. "An hour it is."

Jacob took another look at him. "You said you would change. Do you think you can find time to look a bit more...leaderly?"

"I will make a good show, don't worry." A quick clean-up spell would do the job, and if he glowed as he entered, so be it.

24

Inside the museum, Trahaearn cleared his mind as he descended to the workroom. He couldn't be worried about meetings, or videos, or anything for that matter if he was going to create a godlike being out of thin air.

"Wait," Lionel shouted.

When had he arrived? "I need peace, Lionel."

"No, you need us." He stepped aside and Dionne started down the stairs.

"It's not time for everyone to help. I need to do this alone."

Dionne gave him a gentle shove. "Keep going, druid. You need us. I've done all the research I can on this Shiva guy. I'll help you with that, and Lionel can keep Kali busy while we get her trapped."

Druids were much more obedient than witches. "Kali will try to turn you to her side. If I am the only one there, she cannot cause trouble."

Lionel moved the ingredients for the spell from the side of the room to the center. "You can't create Shiva and talk to Kali at the same time."

"And what does Quinn think of you participating?"

Dionne chuckled. "He doesn't like it, but we aren't his apprentices, so he couldn't do much." She handed Trahaearn a circle of rope twined with charms. "Put this on." She reached into the top of her blouse and pulled out an identical rope necklace. "It will keep her from accessing our minds. It's not permanent, but we should be okay for the duration of the spell."

There was no time for him to argue them out of the room and he didn't think ordering them would work. They were right. He would have to draw the circle to entice Kali and create her lover at the same time. He had a plan, but there was more certainty in numbers.

He hung the rope charm around his neck. "Okay. If we succeed, Quinn won't have anything to complain about and if we fail... Well, we can only be killed once."

He directed Dionne to create the Kali circle, leaving an opening. That would stop the magic from activating until they were ready.

"Lionel, you draw a simple power circle outside Dionne's work. We'll close the inner circle as soon as we have Shiva. You stay outside in case we need to call for assistance."

The two worked fast. Within moments, Trahaearn felt the slight pressure of Lionel's circle press on him. He and Dionne were now safe from interference. Looking up he could see that Lionel wasn't happy to be outside, but there was no room for three in this spell.

He watched Dionne move smoothly to draw the intricate pattern. She was using black salt and the pattern lay on the dark soil. Barely any contrast between salt and soil made it seem to him that both were part of a larger pattern. "Wait," he said more sharply than he'd intended. "Don't forget to leave a gap."

Dionne didn't look up from her work as she answered, "I will, but the smaller the gap, the faster we can close it."

He leaned over as she moved aside, hands still clenched around the last of the salt. Dionne had left only a few grains missing from the pattern. "Excellent work. How did you learn that?"

She shrugged. "I just thought it would work. Quinn says I'm good at circles."

He motioned for her to sit in the center of the drawing. "When we have Shiva, close the circle. Kali will be drawn to it, but I'll also invite her."

He took the ingredients that Ceredig left them. There was a short incantation written on a scrap of paper. The only other instruction was to mix the ingredients to a paste while reciting the words until they succeeded. "Let's hope this doesn't take long." He imbued the words with all the hope he could spare.

Dionne glanced at the paper. "Should I repeat the words too?"

"They were written for me. Can you hold them up for me to read?" Another good reason for having someone in there with him. Perhaps it was time to change the druid tradition of isolation.

Trahaearn poured a tiny amount of the spelled water into the palm of his hand, adding the herbs and spices that were on the plate. The mixture filled his hand but would blend easily. He read the words again, setting them in his mind. A nod at Dionne, and Trahaearn started the incantation.

After three repetitions, he felt another presence enter the circle. It seemed to coalesce out of the air. Whatever it was remained invisible. Trahaearn kept repeating the spell until he heard a gentle voice in his mind.

"I am here."

"Shiva?" He couldn't risk that someone else had been created.

"Yes, that is what I am called in this realm." There was wonder and confidence in the voice.

"And you know what we need?"

"I do, and this is not the first time I have been called to act in this role."

How did he know that? Hoping that they hadn't made a huge

mistake, Trahaearn closed his hand around the paste, not wanting to dispel the being by accident.

"Close the circle, Dionne." As soon as she straightened from dropping the last grains in place, he said, "Kali, I invite you to this circle."

The pressure inside increased again, and then Kali faded into sight. She grinned and looked around. "Druid, this is a most pretty circle. Do you wish to use it to declare your adoration of me?"

She seemed unaware of the presence of her lover. "No, I have asked you here to meet someone."

Kali turned slowly around the circle stopping to stare at Dionne. "Is she my sacrifice?"

"Not her, Kali. Lord Shiva is here."

She spun back to face Trahaearn. "I do not know who that is. There is no one else here except you, the sacrifice, and me."

Did she really not know him? Had Trahaearn imagined the twitch of her shoulders when he mentioned the name?

"You are his consort." Trahaearn had no intention of getting into an argument. He'd just provide the facts. He tried not to wonder why Shiva didn't step up, but it niggled in the back of his mind. If Trahaearn had to figure out how to make it work with Shiva, he could make a mistake with Kali. And that mistake could be taking too long. The circle wouldn't hold her forever.

"I am no one's consort. I am Kali. I am the bringer of death. I am the drinker of blood. Mortals quake beneath my feet."

She spun in a circle as she spoke, her clothes bright against the azure of her skin, her jewelry tinkling and glinting. He felt her attention on him. She was no longer aware of Dionne, let alone an invisible being.

"This is only one aspect of you, Kali. You are also the bringer of life."

"That is nothing compared to the power of death. The power of pain, the power of loss." She slowed her twirling and then stopped, facing Trahaearn. "I will have you groveling at my feet, druid. Then you will understand."

"I will not join you, Kali."

"You will have no choice. That boy outside this protection is ripe for me to take. Would you like a demonstration?"

Trahaearn felt Dionne move to protect Lionel and patted the soil to signal her to stay. "I have seen your demonstrations. Glen only accused me for his own ambition. He did not praise you."

Kali slid her gaze to Dionne. "Perhaps the girl?"

"No. Kali, listen to me. You will not survive if everyone is dead." Was she incapable of thinking beyond the next feeding?

A cruel smile broke on her face, then her tongue slipped through her lips, as though she was lapping up the power in the room.

Kali reached out her hand and beckoned Dionne to her side.

Dionne didn't move.

Kali paled. "You are protected." She leaned toward Dionne. "It will not last forever. Come to me now, and I will be kind."

Dionne raised an eyebrow. "I'm pretty sure we define kind differently. You have no power in this place. Listen to Trahaearn if you wish to survive."

Kali spun back to face Trahaearn. "I have power everywhere, druid. I will return when I am ready to take you."

Trahaearn watched as she reached for something invisible. A frown creased her brow. She waved her hands in front of her face. "How are you keeping me here?"

He wondered the same thing. The circle was supposed to attract her attention and only work as long as she found it pretty. Kali had not looked at the design since she entered.

He wasn't the one keeping her here.

25

The veil was gone.

Kali reached for it, but it was gone. What had the druid done to trap her? She could see the wizard on the outside of the circle, the plain one, not the beautiful one they had drawn for her. If the witch weren't protected, Kali would tear her spirit from that body for the power to leave. She turned back to the druid and reached for his spirit but hit the same barrier. They were all protected.

"Let me go, druid." She tried to make it a command, but her energy was draining. She felt cold, and her voice was thin. The cries of old women as they died sounded like that.

"I am not holding you, Kali. I think it is Shiva."

"Do not mention that name." The first time he'd said it the name didn't draw up any memories. Now, it was as though she only had to reach past the first moment she remembered and he would be there.

"Your legend —."

"I do not have a legend!" She heard the shriek in her voice and felt the drain of energy that anger took from her.

"What is happening to you?" the witch asked. "Are you ill? I am a healer."

"Stupid child. I cannot be healed." But there was something numbing her. The heat she'd carried from the beginning was dying out.

The druid reached for her. "We do not wish you to die, Kali."

The thought pierced Kali's chest like a dagger. She remembered the fear. If she failed what would happen? Would she die? Would she be exiled on a different world? These creatures were soft. Perhaps she could disarm them with pity. "I am hungry. If I do not feed, I will pass." The words came out pathetically. She tried to believe that was in her control but feared that it was true emotion. Kali did not beg. "I need deaths."

"You cannot have death. I will not provide you with the bloodshed you desire."

The druid's words were cruel, but Kali could see by the way his spirit hardened that he was unmovable. If she couldn't have their spirits and she couldn't leave, then she was going to die.

Something else was here with them, a being that she hadn't noticed before. Kali turned to where her mind knew someone stood. A tiny point of light was the only evidence of a presence.

"I will have your spirit." She could feel the power of it. If she could have that power, she would live forever no matter what the druid did to her.

The light grew and pulsed. It was pure white, pure energy.

She reached out a hand, the others forgotten in her desire for this being. "I am dying. Feed me." There was no command in her voice. She had no energy to spare. Looking at the hand reaching for the light, she could see through it.

"You will no longer feed on death alone, Kali." The voice was warm. She felt herself drift toward it, her body craving the heat.

"I can only feed on death," she whispered.

"No. You have forgotten who you are." The light formed into a tall column.

Kali turned away from the brilliance. Something was gnawing at her spirit. Was it a memory? Or simply the hunger?

"Look at me, Kali, and remember."

She bowed her head and covered her eyes. "I will not. There is nothing to remember."

"Look at me."

She felt the gentle touch of fingers on her arm. It brought a flood of shame to reheat her body. It didn't last. She could see through her fingers. The druid was smiling at her and pointing for her to look again at the light.

Fear tore her heart apart. "I cannot."

The being trailed his fingers down her arm to the elbow before removing them. A memory of before slipped into her mind like a snake; light and beauty everywhere, joyful dancing and song. Love.

"Look at me, Kali, and remember!" The voice left no room for disobedience.

Kali turned and saw a man, tall, dark hair falling in curls to his waist. A smile on his lips that said welcome, and forgiveness, and love.

"I remember," she said. Tendrils of power wrapped around her ankles and wrists, but they didn't come from Shiva. The air flowed with the energy of death, birth, passion, and love. All of it flowed through her, requiring no energy to draw. It fed her.

"Druid, I thank you for returning my consort to me," Shiva said. Then he took Kali's arm and they faded through the veil together.

"Wait," Trahaearn called to the empty air. He couldn't just leave it at that, life on this side still needed to go on.

A tiny spark of light blinked on. "What do you wish to ask?" The words appeared in his mind.

He looked at Dionne and then at Lionel. If he could only get one answer it must be something that helped build harmony between the humans and magical folk.

"What will happen now? Will Kali still fight us?" It was stupidly put, but the best he could do.

"You will have a new goddess of death and fertility. I know that Kali has been a trial, but she is not just the goddess of life and death. She brings change. I feel that your world has changed, so perhaps you will be more lucky."

The light pulsed.

"Can I ask a question?" Dionne said.

"One, and then I must leave."

"Are you really a god?"

Trahaearn held his breath. For all of the druid knowledge, he'd sounded more confident to Angela than he felt when he explained the connection between the human gods and these beings.

"A god is many things, child. Humans are not the only creatures who worship gods. Other worlds have other names for us... me..." The light went out and the words in Trahaearn's mind faded.

"Clear the circles," he said, rising from the dirt. "We still have work to do."

Dionne broke the design at the same time Lionel created a gap in the outer circle.

"Did you hear everything?" she asked Lionel.

"Yes," he said picking up a broom to sweep the salt aside. "What happens if we get another maniac like Kali?"

Dionne held out her left hand and the black salt rose out of the soil to gather in her right hand. She did the same with the plain salt from the outer circle. Trahaearn made a note to get her to teach the spell to the druids. It saved hours of sifting salt from dirt. And if her skills in creating spells from need were a result of her upbringing as a human, the world of magic was about to undergo a renaissance.

"I need you to work with Allun and Ceredig to seek out the new goddess while I am gone." Trahaearn wiped his hands on his robes. "I need to get ready."

Dionne started up the stairs and then turned back after looking at her phone. "You've got about fifteen minutes."

❧ 26 ❧

They had been talking all day. Trahaearn was exhausted and if anyone asked him to show them more magic, he'd have to draw power from the earth. That would entail a twenty-floor elevator ride. How did humans manage to be so far from the earth?

It was his turn to speak to the group, or rather to the crowd of reporters and microphones. He'd learned a lot about how humans communicated in the last eighteen hours, and Jacob had prepared his speech. It was just a formality. The agreements had been made and signed. They'd turned it into oaths in a surprise gesture to the magical community — that was the name that everyone, well, all the humans, had confirmed as the least provocative name. Trahaearn knew that there was a myriad of details to work through to make the world safe for every kind of being, but those details would come from a base of understanding and trust.

Trahaearn stood, smoothed the robes he'd worn for the ceremony and approached the microphones. As he passed, Jacob nodded approval and gave him a quick thumbs up. It was good to get the approval, but all Trahaearn wanted to do was sleep. He summoned the dregs of energy he needed, knowing this was the last thing he had to accomplish before he could reach for replenishment.

"It is with great optimism that I announce this agreement for the magical community," he said while wondering how the magical community all over the world was going to find out about it as quickly as the humans. "We have planted the seeds today for a harmonious relationship between those of us who are able to touch the energies that allow us to do magic, and those of us who are grounded in the practical world. I look forward to a time when we can work together to make a bright future for us and our children."

The reporters chuckled at the term bright future. Jacob had suggested that it would lighten the mood, but Trahaearn thought it too obvious since he was emitting so much light from the magic he'd performed.

"As you can imagine, my colleagues and I have worked hard to gain an understanding of the impacts of this new world. We will continue to work hard to implement the laws and relationships that will allow the understanding to grow."

A few hands went up. He knew there would be questions, but he hoped they would be simple. It wouldn't look good for him to constantly admit he didn't know the answer. A druid always had an answer.

After the questions, most of which were presented to the humans, and the farewells to the leaders, Trahaearn followed the two security agents from the room. Jacob caught up as they stood in front of the elevator.

"It went better than anyone hoped," Jacob said. "I heard from Dionne, she says the others agreed to the arrangements, and will abide by your oaths. Does that mean no one from the magical community will be able to coerce a human with magic?"

Trahaearn nodded. "I need energy, but then we'll convene the council and formalize the agreement. Don't make the mistake of thinking there will be no problems, Jacob. The magical folk are just as capable of interpreting the rules to their advantage as any human."

The doors to the hotel opened, and the taste of unfiltered air refreshed Trahaearn. "I need to get to the soil before we do anything else."

The security team led them to a small park across from the hotel and stood arms crossed and exuding menace in their attitude. Removing his shoes, Trahaearn sank his feet into the manicured lawn to feel the deep warm power of the soil. He felt it flow in his veins, pulse in his tattoos, and light up his spirit.

After a few minutes, he pulled on his shoes, feeling whole again. "We need to get to the museum."

THE ENTIRE COUNCIL SAT AROUND THE DINNER TABLE IN THE kitchen of the museum. Maeve, accompanied by two of her courtiers, represented the sidhe. Beacon, bent almost in half to fit in the room, spoke for all the forest creatures. Mark rested his bulk on a bench, since there were no chairs able to fit a troll. Although not part of the council, Queen Bud stood on the table, to represent the entirety of the fairies. The final representatives of the magical community were Quinn, Lionel, and Dionne. They represented the witches and wizards.

Trahaearn didn't want the position of leader, he wanted to simply be the Arch Druid and allow everyone to make their own way, but he knew that the days of isolation for druids was long past. If they hadn't been so fond of retreating from the world, perhaps the vampires would not have succeeded in taking over this grove. It would take time, but he knew that someone had to lead the other beings into a working relationship with humans, someone who could protect the humans as much as the magical folk.

Beacon was the first to voice his question, "Now that everyone knows the details, and we've all agreed to the conditions, what are we to do next?"

"Yes," Maeve added. "How are we to thrive in this new world you have concocted?"

Just like the sidhe to avoid responsibility for anything that didn't work completely in their favor.

Trahaearn stood so everyone would hear him. "The answers are out there, with the humans. We have Dionne who can work as an ambassador. She has knowledge of the way humans think. We have allies in Jacob and Angela. Others will come forward. It will not happen overnight, but we will find a place in their world. And they will find a place in ours."

Mark shifted on his bench and was about to say something when the air became heavy, and the light from the candles flickered.

No one moved.

Trahaearn didn't know if it was shock, or a spell that held them in place. He tried to open his mouth to speak, but his body wasn't responding to his brain.

Could they not have a moment's breathing space? What disaster was crashing down on them now?

A wisp of smoke curled in the air above the center of the table. It thickened and grew into the form of a woman. Then the smoke faded and details of the woman sharpened, pale skin, almost translucent, dark thick hair that hung to her waist. Deep green eyes, like the sea just before a storm, focused on Trahaearn.

"This will be interesting, druid." A low voice vibrated along his nerves as though he were a harp.

"Who are you?" He knew the answer before she spoke. It could only be one person.

"I am Arianrhod. Kali sends her good wishes."

What did one say to a goddess? "Welcome."

"I see fear in your spirit, druid. Why?"

Trahaearn held himself as still as possible, not wanting to react until he knew this being better. If she was a danger, then he would have to prepare for yet another battle. "It is unsettling to face so many of your kind in such a short time."

Arianrhod chuckled. "Do you fear that I am another goddess of death?"

"Death is not the worst thing," Trahaearn said. "I worry that you are not balanced between life and death. That our world is in danger."

"I am not like Kali. I plan to stay here forever. I want the humans to believe in me, not to quake in terror at my name. I want you, and those like to you to thrive. This world will be better for me if that happens."

Relief wrapped warm arms around him. "We have the same goal, Arianrhod, I look forward to a long and fruitful future for all of us."

The woman faded back into smoke and then the world started again.

WANT MORE?

Five years after the prophecy a sprite and a fairy join forces to become private investigators. Us the QR code to join the team in Blood Magic Blues and discover the truth behind the case.

Sneak peek next.

If you enjoyed reading DRUID, please consider helping other readers to find the story by leaving a review.

CHAPTER 1

F ernlight looked around the office space. Bramble was flitting from the corner of the desk to the bookshelf and back. Opening a business was risky; doing it as the first sprite private detective added a layer of uncertainty that human businesses didn't have. Partnering with a fairy would at least make it interesting.

Bramble settled for a moment on one of the client chairs. "When will our first customer come in?"

He was currently in his natural state, about three feet tall with visible wings. When he'd first approached Fernlight, she'd been reluctant to take on a fairy. They were short-lived and had short attention spans. But he'd convinced her that their goals were the same: to make a place in the human world. Bramble's clan had no power in the fairy world, and he was determined to change that.

"Client," she said. "They are called clients. And I don't know. We did what Dionne said; posted on social media and made a website. But that doesn't mean people will knock on our door on day one. Especially since it's almost closing time."

His eyes lost focus for a moment and a glamor slid into place. Now the wings were gone, and he looked to be closer to five feet tall. "Now I'm dressed for business. And it's not my fault we had to wait for the furniture."

No, she'd been the one to order the desks and chairs. "I know."

"We need to make something happen," he said. "I don't have the time for us to sit around waiting. I need to make my name now!"

Fernlight sighed. "You've been reading those inspirational posts on Facebook again."

"Twitter; I think that's more fun," he said.

She couldn't argue his point. Sprites were long-lived beings — people; she must remember that they were now considered people because it made the humans more comfortable — so she was patient, but perhaps the business needed a boost. Perhaps their agency needed to be more like a fairy than a sprite right now.

"What about doing some networking?" she asked. "See if there are any business groups we could join."

He hopped the desk to sit in his chair. Bramble's desk was near the east wall and Fernlight's desk near the west. It looked open, but they had a privacy spell that could separate the two areas when needed. The desk was metal and glass, the chairs plastic, the floor terracotta tile. No wood was wasted on furniture.

"You look nice," Bramble said as he typed. Another annoying trait. He didn't always answer her question if he had something to say.

Dionne, Quinn Larson's apprentice and one of the six beings who brought about the prophecy, had taken up the challenge of helping Real Folk blend better with humans. She'd outright ordered Fernlight to get some business suits and work clothes. Sprites were more likely to spend their time in loose clothes when they weren't naked in the forest.

Fernlight smoothed the side of the dress she wore. It was moss green and matched her eyes. She would put on the jacket when they had a client, to increase the businessperson effect. The flat shoes were less uncomfortable each time she put them on; barefoot was another no-no. At over six feet tall she wouldn't need the added stature of heels, thank the spirits.

"Why would that work?" Bramble asked. He clicked the mouse and kept searching.

Dionne had explained this as well. Fernlight was getting used to repeating information to Bramble enough times that he remembered. It wasn't everything, and it was irritating, because if he heard something that interested him, he never forgot it.

"People will know us, and then when they have a problem, or a friend has one, they'll come to our agency."

"We could go for afternoon coffee with this mastermind group," Bramble said, turning the computer so she could read the screen.

"It says they are a knitting group." She pointed to the heading on the page.

"Does that mean they won't need something investigated?" Bramble sat with his fingers poised over the keyboard. "What should I look for? Do you think there's a group called, 'people who need private investigators'?"

Fernlight shook her head and moved to her own desk. The effort it took to answer Bramble's questions was much higher than the effort to do the research herself, even with her lack of skills. "Business people like us might be better."

"Why?"

Good question. This morning she'd felt optimistic, happy to start the business, looking forward to helping people find lost relatives, or catch someone doing wrong. But the *idea* of having a business was very different from actually running one. Despite her earlier words, she had held a tiny hope that someone would just walk in the door as soon as the sign was unveiled. The Magic Search Agency didn't need much clarification.

"I don't know," she said in answer to Bramble's questions. "What do you think?"

Bramble sat back in his chair. "I think we should try to meet as many people as we can. We don't know who will need our help. And it will be fun." The last words trailed off. Bramble, like most fairies, was afraid of humans. He'd sworn that it wouldn't get in the way, that he was going to be the first fairy who could handle humans, but there was still some trepidation in his voice.

"Hello." The front door opened, and a young human woman stepped into the office. "Are you open?"

Bramble froze, despite his efforts to overcome his fear. So Fernlight stood and reached out her hand to shake with this first client. "Yes, this is our first day. I'm Fernlight." She gestured to Bramble and introduced him. The woman shook Fernlight's hand and waved at Bramble.

"I'm Bella," she said. "I run the cafe next door? Vegan Victuals?" Every sentence was a question.

"How can we help you?" Fernlight said,

"Oh. No, I'm not here to hire you. I'm offering you help. We have a small business community group and we all try to help out." Bella smiled and then pointed at Fernlight's arm. "I love your tattoos, by the way."

Running her finger along her skin, Fernlight said, "That's my skin, not a tattoo." Unlike Bella, who had very pale skin that contrasted with her bright red hair, Fernlight had white hair that grew in short spikes and skin the color of Arbutus bark with faint grain lines.

Bella blushed. "I'm so sorry. I've never met a sprite before."

Fernlight pointed to the client chairs. "No need to apologize. Tell us about this community group."

As she turned to follow Bella, Fernlight noticed a man standing outside the office, staring into the window. He looked angry and she hoped he was simply waiting for a friend, and not the first of a group of protesters. Some humans still wouldn't accept that magic was normal.

The man was standing outside.

Just like a human to be weird. Bramble turned away from his surveillance of the possible attacker and glanced at Fernlight. It was too hard to keep his thoughts on the human when his partner was sitting there with another one. He tried not to be afraid. He remembered what Fernlight said, that the humans were not going to hurt him. It did help a bit, but it was still hard to keep his eyes on both threats.

"When is the next meeting?" He heard Fernlight ask the female.

Were they going to a meeting with lots of humans? How was he going to keep them safe? He expected to have time to prepare for that. His heart fluttered, and the room began to spin.

Bramble placed his hands on the desk to stop the room spinning. If he couldn't manage one human nearby and one outside, Fernlight wouldn't let him be her partner. If that happened, his family would fade into the shadows of fairy life. His only chance to improve his standing with the other fairy tribes was to be the first to successfully work with humans face-to-face. To even help them.

Dionne had known what would happen. She worked with lots of fairies, so she knew how hard it was to not be afraid. Bramble closed his eyes and imagined how life would be for his grandchildren. It would use up his whole life to make them important; this was for the future. The happy image of a large tribe of Bramble fairies slowed his heart and steadied the room.

When he felt safe, he opened his eyes and let go of the desk. His heart sped up again.

The man was opening the door!

Bramble looked to where Fernlight was still talking to the

female human. She gave him the look. That stare. The one that meant, this is your chance to prove your worth. Or maybe just meant, say hello and ask the man to wait.

Bramble poured a little more energy into the glamor, making himself an inch taller, then stood up and walked to the man.

"Welcome to the Magic Search Agency," Bramble said. He was proud that his voice didn't shake, but decided it might be better if it wasn't so squeaky. "What can we do to help you?" The baritone voice rumbled pleasantly in his chest.

The human took a step back. That was a surprise. Maybe he didn't like deep voices.

"I am Agent Bramble." This time it was a higher voice, but it gave the man twitches around his mouth. "Do you need something investigated?"

Now the human showed his teeth. Bramble took two steps back. The man was getting ready to eat him!

The man closed his lips. Perhaps he wasn't going to eat them yet.

"I am Mamoru Yamana," he said. "I want to engage your services."

Their first customer! Bramble felt his wings start to push through the glamor in his excitement. "Come to my desk. I will listen to your request and then my partner will join us."

The man looked at Fernlight and the woman then back at the desk Bramble pointed to.

"This is confidential," he said.

"Yes, come and tell me what you need," Bramble said, pointing again to his client seat.

The man shook his head. "I need privacy. I will return when you have no other clients."

No!

Bramble wanted their first client to be his. It didn't matter that it was a human. He wasn't scared anymore. He was excited. And Fernlight would know how valuable a partner he was.

"The other human will not hear us," Bramble said. Now his voice was too high, the man winced. He knew humans could only hear some voices, and fairies could hear and speak outside those ranges. He tried to calm himself. He looked around to see what the man saw. Oh no! He'd forgotten to put up the privacy spell. "Look," he said waving the spell into action.

The man raised an eyebrow as a wall of tree trunks appeared between the desks. Fernlight had chosen the appearance and refused to make it a wall of brambles when he made the suggestion.

"Come, sit, and you will see that we cannot hear them." Bramble wanted to pull the man to the chair, but he wasn't quite ready to touch a human.

The man stepped forward, not to the chair, but to the wall. He reached out to press his fingers against it, then pulled them back as they sank into the trees. "Impressive."

Bramble grinned and wanted to flit around the room, but he knew that would not be the way a serious agent would behave. "Sit. Let's get your information on the file."

His client pulled the chair out and sat.

Success!

While the human settled, Bramble opened a notebook and selected a pen from the twenty he had in his drawer. Each one was a different color, and he thought it would look good to have files in different colors too.

"Before we start a file," the human said. "I want to know more about your experience with investigations."

Bramble almost said, 'we don't have any' when he remembered that he was not supposed to say things like that. He was supposed to say things to make their customer... no no no, client... comfortable. They had talked about this because Fernlight said humans would want to be sure that they were hiring someone who would help.

"We use our special skills to find answers," he said. It didn't sound right to him. Was he supposed to be enthusiastic about it? It wasn't a lie, not that he had a problem with lying to humans, or anyone for that matter.

"How have you used those skills?"

Bramble's mind froze up. He'd said the words they'd agreed, and it hadn't worked. What should he say next? Maybe they should have made up a case so they could show how great they were at investigation.

Bramble could feel his glamor slipping as he struggled to think of an answer.

Then, the human woman walked past following Fernlight to the door. It felt like a lifetime, but as soon as they were alone, Fernlight canceled the privacy spell and sat beside the human.

FERNLIGHT JOINED BRAMBLE AND THE HUMAN. AS SHE DID, Bramble's body stopped trembling and relaxed into his usual fidgety mode. At least this time he hadn't gone catatonic.

"I'm Fernlight," she said. "This is Bramble, we are the lead investigators. How can we help you?"

The man smoothed his suit and then placed his hands in his lap. His posture straightened even more. Fernlight had never seen a human sit so straight.

"I am Mr. Yamana. Mamoru Yamana," he said. "I believe I may need to hire you to solve a particular problem."

He didn't elaborate and Fernlight understood Bramble's reaction. They could follow their prepared scripts all day, but if the client wouldn't share, nothing would happen.

"If you can tell us a little?" She made it a question because she'd noticed that humans seemed compelled to answer questions.

"I require you to keep this confidential."

Fernlight gave Bramble a glance. He returned it with a glare as if there were no chance of him blabbing secrets.

"You have our word," she replied. "But if that is not enough, you can sign a client agreement, and then you'll have our liability." The online sales classes that Bramble had found suggested this as a closing tactic; get the client committed early.

Mr. Yamana tugged at his sleeves before speaking. "I would prefer we sign an agreement. It is not so much for me, but this case is too important to leave anything to chance."

Fernlight nodded to Bramble and he printed the form. This Mr. Yamana was taking a chance on them. It would not do to be offended by his professionalism.

When Bramble placed the form and a pen on the desk, Fernlight held out her hand to him. "The spell."

Bramble started and then blushed. "Sorry, I forgot." He opened a locked cupboard and pulled out a twist of parchment.

"Mr. Yamana," Fernlight said. "Signing the form is one level of protection for you. I am sure the humans would find that sufficient."

He nodded, but the wry smile told a different story.

"With Real Folk," she continued, "we can improve on that. This spell will make it impossible for us to discuss the case without your permission. Or by applying the oath to that person."

"Interesting," he said, tapping the pen against the paper. "What is required?"

The first hurdle over — most humans were still suspicious of magic — Fernlight opened the parchment. "We say these words and burn the paper and its contents. You will add a permission word at the end."

"Very well," he said.

"The form goes first," Bramble said. "It anchors the spell."

Fernlight placed her hand on the desk, their signal that Bramble should stop speaking. Without it, the fairy would likely go off on a tangent and tell four or five stories about similar spells.

Mr. Yamana signed and passed the form to Fernlight. When all signatures were completed, she placed the contents of the parchment in an ashtray and gave their very first client the script of the spell.

"Do you have a permission word? It should be something you wouldn't accidentally say, but not so weird that people would know something is up, and you could say it when strangers are around, and they wouldn't know you were doing anything, and it should be simple..."

His nerves were making him ramble despite her signals. Fernlight touched Bramble's hand. The fairy snapped his mouth shut.

Mr. Yamana's mouth twitched with a suppressed smile. "I will use the word, persimmon. It is in season, so it will not be odd to speak the word. I do not care for them, so I am unlikely to say it by accident."

When Mr. Yamana nodded that he was ready, Fernlight lit the small heap of herbs and twigs in the ashtray, and all three recited the spell. As soon as Mr. Yamana spoke his permission word, Fernlight took the parchment from him and tossed it on the embers of the ingredients. A sudden flame consumed the parchment and remaining ashes in a fire so hot it left nothing but a curl of smoke.

"I feel different," Mr. Yamana said. "As though I would know where you are even without seeing you."

Bramble picked up the ashtray and moved it to the side of the desk. "Yes, that is part of the spell. It will fade a little as time passes and we will undo it when the case is solved, and you won't need to worry, we are just connected now, and there's no..."

This time Fernlight stopped Bramble with a look.

She turned back to their client. "Mr. Yamana."

"Mamoru, please. We are connected so it seems impolite to use such formalities."

She nodded. "If you will tell us about the case, and why you chose us."

He unbuttoned his jacket and relaxed. The movement turned him from a stiff cold human to a friendlier, more open one. Fernlight tucked that knowledge away for use in the future. Human body language was still a gray area for most Real Folk.

"I think it will be apparent why I came to you, when I explain the case. But first, you must know that I work for the Human Occult Protection Department, in the investigation bureau."

Fernlight glared at Bramble to keep him from responding. HOP-D, as everyone seemed to call it, was supposed to protect both humans and Real Folk, but mostly it seemed to side with humans. "I would think you have all the investigative power you need."

Mamoru shifted in his chair. "It is not the power, but a difference of opinion on... shall we call it perspective? A case I was working on proved difficult, and despite the potential for severe damage to both humans and magical folk, I have been told to end my investigation."

"So, you came to us to keep your work going?" Fernlight understood the rationale, but HOP-D would not let them simply look into a case they had deemed closed.

"Not exactly," Mamoru said. "I think I was close. I want you to find someone. If I can prove... Well, there are rumors of a drug that allows humans to do magic. If you can find proof, and one person who is using the drug, I can open the investigation again."

"And then HOP-D can blame us?" Bramble rose from his chair in indignation, his glamor slipping away.

CHAPTER 2

This was more than Fernlight had planned. Her first client was supposed to be easy; a lost pet, or a cheating spouse. A quick spell and then the agency would have some successes to use in marketing. That was what Dionne told them would be best. Now this man was asking her to work with an organization that had a reputation for blaming Real Folk for everything. And Bramble was beyond calming.

"I think we need to think about this," she said, keeping her eye on Bramble to make sure she could interrupt any explosion. "HOP-D is not what we envisioned as our first client."

Mamoru held up his hand. "I understand, but please let me be clear. I alone am your client, not my employer. I will be able to keep your involvement confidential."

He waited for Fernlight to respond. When she didn't, Mamoru stood. "When can I expect an answer? I must remind you of the urgency. If this drug is real, and it becomes popular, it will make the relations between humans and magical beings worse, not better."

Bramble was starting to sink back into the chair. His wings slowing to a blur of motion. "We understand. No human can simply take on magic and hope to survive. We will let you know tomorrow morning."

Mamoru didn't argue, but by the way his face had become expressionless again and his body rigid, he wasn't happy. He pulled a card from his pocket, held it in two hands to present to her. "I will wait for your call."

The back of the card faced Fernlight. A phone number printed across the blank space. When she flipped it over, the HOP-D logo seemed to jump out at her.

Fernlight watched until Mamoru was through the door and across the street. Bramble was still silent, but he had returned his glamor and was sitting in the chair, not floating above it. She was aware of the flicker of his heartbeat at the edge of her sprite senses; it was slower, but still fueled with emotion.

"We need more information," she said to forestall his immediate refusal.

"It's a trick," he grumbled. Then he started typing searches into the computer.

Fernlight would do a little magic research while Bramble used his skills in the electronic world. He'd surprised her with his skill when they'd learned of the internet. Perhaps it was his scattered fairy nature that made Bramble so capable with the computer. When she tried to do the same research, she found it too hard to discern real from fantasy.

"We can, at least, find out if Mamoru is telling the truth. And, perhaps, it is a trap for him, rather than for us."

"That won't matter," Bramble said without looking at her. "HOP-D will be happy to arrest Real Folk."

She sighed. There was no point in arguing until they had more facts. "I'll be right here." She pointed at the floor in front of the desk. The spell would work better if she was closer to where Mamoru had been. "I'll lock the door. If anyone comes, pull me out of the trance."

Bramble nodded, still typing rapidly.

Fernlight ignored her worries. She had agreed to partner with Bramble for a reason. She had to start trusting that he would take things seriously and not get lost in his research, emotions, or new interesting things that happened.

Fernlight kept a handful of the sunflower seeds that held the truth spell in her desk. Despite advice from the wizard who had sold them to her, she would not use them on humans without permission; it set a bad precedent. In the future, she'd make it part of the contract process. She'd been sure that any lie a human told would be easy to see. Now, she wasn't so confident.

Taking the matches and burn bowl from the desk, she lowered herself to the tiled floor. Dropping one seed into the burn bowl, she slipped into the light trance needed to focus her energy. It wasn't necessary to burn the seeds for the spell, but it made her feel better that no human could get them by accident and be hurt by any residual magic.

If Mamoru was right, then she needed to be far more careful. What if the drug worked, and then humans were able to pick up discarded spell ingredients? Even a trace of magic could cause damage in untrained hands.

Fernlight took the seed, held it tightly in her right fist and spoke the words of the spell. "If untruths have been uttered here, display them."

If Mamoru had lied, the words would float across the air.

Nothing happened.

When they'd stocked up on charms like this, Fernlight had expected that humans would be similar to Real Folk. That there was an underlying trust in the way the world worked. Now she knew it was naive to believe that. The lack of results didn't make her feel satisfied. It made her feel like they had been tricked. No matter what she said to Bramble, the mention of HOP-D stirred fear in her too.

She placed the sunflower seed in the burn bowl and lit the match. It took longer than the contract spell to burn, and it filled the office with the odor of burned oil. When all that was left was ashes, she rose, opened the door and coaxed the air to blow a cleansing breeze.

Bramble was still tapping at keys, but now there were printouts on the desk beside him. By the light outside she had been in the trance for an hour. It was almost time to lock the door and leave.

"Any luck?" she asked.

He looked up. "Did he tell the truth?"

Fernlight confirmed the results of the spell. "What did you find?" She reached for the pile of papers.

"You want to take the case," Bramble said, staring at the screen.

Fernlight nodded. "It will be good for the business, but I want to hear your opinions. Bramble, we're partners. If you have a solid reason to say no, then we'll keep looking for another client. I just..."

He closed the lid of his computer. "I know. If we don't take it and the drug works, we'll be responsible for whatever happens."

And that was why she partnered with him. He got to the core of a problem fast. "We still have a choice. We can send Mamoru to the druids."

"Okay, but I thought you wanted to do this," Bramble fluttered to the chair beside her. "I thought I would be too afraid to take the case, but I think we should."

Surprised, Fernlight put the papers on the desk.

"I do, but I think there's more to it than what he told us. We don't know what the internal games are at HOP-D, we don't really know if there is a drug, just that Mamoru believes it."

Bramble waved his hand over the pile of printouts. "There's information in there that says the same as Mamoru, and more, and I don't know why they wanted him to stop the investigation, but I found all the details. The internet is full of things we need to know, and a little fairy magic opens all the files I need."

"So, we tell him yes?" Fernlight touched her middle where a tiny kernel of doubt sat hard and knotted.

"Yes, and we should do it now so we can get started, and he should come back, but I don't think he should know that I got all this. I think humans want to believe their secrets are safe, and I think it would work best for us, and all the Real Folk, if they kept thinking that. Do you want me to call Mamoru? I'm not scared to do it, and I can ask him if he will come back tonight."

Bramble's enthusiasm helped her to ignore the doubt. "I think we can wait until tomorrow to meet him. You go ahead and let Mamoru know we'll take the case and set up an appointment."

Five years after the prophecy a sprite and a fairy join forces to become private investigators. Us the QR code to join the team in Blood Magic Blues and discover the truth behind the case.

FREE EBOOK

Claim your copy of Spells and Other Charms when you use the QR code to sign up for my newsletter and learn more about Quinn and Cate's past.

ALSO BY P A WILSON

For more books by P A Wilson

Use the QR code below or go to pawilson.ca

ABOUT THE AUTHOR

Perry Wilson is a Canadian author based in Vancouver, BC who has big ideas and an itch to tell stories. Having spent some time on university, a career, and life in general, she returned to writing in 2008 and hasn't looked back since (well, maybe a little, but only while parallel parking).

She is a member of the Vancouver Writers Social Group, The Royal City Literary Arts Society, and The Surrey Writing Workshop. Perry has self-published several novels. She writes the Madeline Journeys, a fantasy series about a high-powered lawyer who finds herself trapped in a magical world, the Quinn Larson Quests, which follows the adventures of a wizard named Quinn who must contend with volatile fae in the heart of Vancouver, and the Charity Deacon Investigations, a mystery thriller series about a private eye who tends to fall into serious trouble with her cases, and The Riverton Romances, a series based in a small town in Oregon, one of her favorite states. Her stand-alone novels are Breaking the Bonds, Closing the Circle, and The Dragon at The Edge of The Map.

For more information
www.pawilson.ca
pawilson@pawilson.ca

ACKNOWLEDGMENTS

People think that the process of writing is solitary. That's not the case for me. I have help from so many people it would be hard to acknowledge everyone, but I'll give it a try.

The support and inspiration I get from my writer's groups is incalculable. The Vancouver Writers Social Group opens my mind to other ways of telling a story. The Royal City Literary Arts Society gives me the opportunity to meet and share with other writers who have more knowledge than I do. The Other 11 Months group is where I learn about getting the words on the page. And my critique group who helps me find the best parts of the story I want to tell. Thanks to all of the members of these great groups.

Last of all, but definitely a huge part of the process, my beta readers. These are the people who love stories and are willing, and more than able, to tell me if my finished story is ready for you, my readers.